Author: Tom Knauss
Project Managers: Zach Glazar and Tom Knauss
Editor: Jeff Harkness
Pathfinder Rules Conversion: Michael "Mars" Russell
Art Direction: Casey Christofferson
Layout and Graphic Design: Charles A. Wright
Cover Design: Charles A. Wright
Cover Art: Héctor Rodríguez Antúnez
Interior Art: Héctor Rodríguez Antúnez
Cartography: Robert Altbauer

FROG GOD GAMES
ISBN: 978-1-943067-58-9

TABLE OF CONTENTS

MAIZE AND MONSTERS

*"PLANTS NOURISHED WITH FOULED WATER CAN STILL FEED A VILLAGE.
A GRAIN OF SAND POISONED WITH THE BLOOD OF INNOCENTS CAN KILL A CITY."*

— AN AZTLI PROVERB

Maize and Monsters is an adventure for four 4th- to 6th-level characters that exposes the adventurers to the grim reality that time sometimes exacerbates old wounds rather than healing them. A recent murder in the village of Pilhua proves to be far more than a simple crime of passion as the seeds for this killing were sown during a previous, unsolved mystery that still haunts some residents within the settlement. The characters must wade through a list of suspects and motives that lead them to discover the ugly truth about a heinous crime that spawned a greater evil than even its perpetrators could ever imagine.

ADVENTURE BACKGROUND

In the Caya Grasslands of northern Tehuatl, most people's lives revolve around the cultivation and harvesting of maize. The crop feeds much of the population and is considered by most to be the lifeblood of society. While the cereal grain usually stands as a silent witness to humanity's actions, there are rare occasions where the stain of evil compels the mindless, green stalks to step forward and provide their irrefutable testimony to man's heinousness.

A little more than one year ago, Conto and his younger sister Chipinia spent a lazy afternoon lying in the maizefields just outside their village staring at the clouds moving across the skies. Away from their parents' attentive gaze, the teenagers enjoyed a brief respite of freedom in the seldom visited, remote locale just beyond the outskirts of their settlement, where they indulged in smoking some tobacco and drinking pulque. Unfortunately, the youngsters were not the only ones that day who wished to go unseen and unnoticed. Two local pochtecas named Mixoch and Temilaz had spent the last several years cultivating a lucrative business relationship with Uetzopilli, a Poqoza from south of the Great Canal who smuggles psychedelic mushrooms and other hallucinogens into the village for distribution throughout the area. The wily half-elf excelled at eluding the authorities and hiding his contraband, but the shady and untrustworthy peddler also had a penchant for swindling his customers and making unnecessary enemies.

During his previous visit north of the waterway separating the island, Uetzopilli had sold worthless, rotting mushrooms to the unscrupulous merchants for a handsome price. The slight proved too much for the pair to ignore after their commercial partner's previous shortcomings and false promises had worn their patience to the bone. The duo naturally hid their displeasure and lured Uetzopilli back to their village under the pretense of partaking in another profitable deal with him. When he arrived at the rendezvous site outside their village, Mixoch and Temilaz's handiwork awaited him. After a few minutes of idle banter and chatter, the startled Uetzopilli quickly came to the realization that something was terribly amiss as he spoke with the duo who were resting their weary arms on their uictlis. When the two men stepped forward, the half-elf suddenly found himself staring into the gaping hole they had dug in the isolated maizefield before his anticipated arrival. In his dangerous line of work, even the naïve Uetzopilli knew what came next, but an unexpected surprise awaited the three conspirators.

The argument and pleas for mercy roused the two youngsters from their tenuous slumber and beckoned them to investigate the transaction further. At first, the teenagers prudently remained quiet and still. However, when the vicious Mixoch thrust his tecpatl into Uetzopilli's abdomen and punctured his heart, the siblings simultaneously shrieked in horror. The shocked murderers momentarily stared at the children's scared faces and instinctually realized the steps they must take to maintain their silence. The wicked pair instantly recognized Conto and Chipinia from the village, and the frightened siblings also knew the killers' identities, marking them for death as well. The panicked 15- and 14-year-olds froze in their tracks, giving Mixoch and Temilaz ample opportunity to pounce on their tragic, innocent witnesses and quickly slay them like livestock for slaughter. The two criminals also tossed their limp, lifeless bodies into the hole along with Mixoch's broken tecpatl and frantically shoveled dirt back into the abscess as if despoiled earth could erase the stains of their sins from the land. The bloodletting lasted less than one minute, but within those 60 seconds, the devious pochtecas had sown the seeds for the terror that would later befall the village.

Naturally, Conto and Chipinia's disappearance prompted an outcry from the children's distraught family and fellow villagers, but an exhaustive search revealed nothing. Mixoch and Temilaz covered their tracks well, at least for now. Evidence of their gruesome crimes eluded investigators, and as days dragged into weeks and then into months, the terrible memories faded and life returned to normal for almost everyone except the children's grieving immediate family members. Yet the secluded gravesite and its occupants refused to rest in peace. The children's innocent blood gave birth to and fed a fearsome terror that soon took root in the increasingly overgrown maizefield. One year later, Conto and Chipinia's restless spirits awoke from their uneasy slumber and plunged their homeland into despair.

ADVENTURE SYNOPSIS

The characters arrive in the small Aztli village of Pilhua in the southern portion of the Caya Grasslands roughly 80 miles due north of the central causeway spanning the Great Canal. One year has passed since the tragic killings, and the consequences of this event are now reaching their fruition. The youngsters' innocent blood transformed the surrounding maize stalks into wahuapas, malevolent maizefolk who prey on the living. These sentient creatures are easily mistaken for ordinary plants, a trait they use to their maximum benefit while they steadily transform the wild grasses into a self-contained maze-like compound by manipulating the plants' growth into a shape and design of their own bizarre creation. Over the past year, the monsters have slowly expanded their range closer to the village where they have now begun to exact their vengeance on the villagers, claiming their first victim just the night before the adventure unfolds.

Heroes drawn into these events must first unmask a wahuapa (maizefolk) as the culprit behind the village's first killing and also untangle the other facets of this complex situation. In the year since Conto and Chipinia's untimely death, the young man's prospective bride Ciahuatl has not forgotten her betrothed. She made a pact with the cihuateteo, the malevolent spirits of women who died in childbirth, to give her the power to avenge his death, which she firmly believes came at the hands of another villager. Later that evening, the cacalotls she breathed to life also descend on the settlement, requiring the characters to intervene to save innocent lives. Meanwhile, Uetzopilli's reanimated corpse actively seeks out his killers, though the undead monstrosity stops at nothing in his quest to exact his brutal brand of frontier justice. After resolving these simultaneous machinations and while gathering more clues in the process, the characters come to the conclusion that the tragic events now plaguing Pilhua all stem from the murders that took place more than one year earlier.

With this knowledge in hand, the characters trek out into the substantially altered maizefield where Conto and Chipinia met their tragic end. The unrequited siblings manipulated the landscape to create a seemingly impossible structure of twisted vegetation and hardened cornstalks that form a contorted maze. The heroes must navigate their way through this treacherous complex of deadly traps, hideous guardians, and grisly sights until they arrive at the makeshift gravesite where the children's remarkably well-preserved bodies still lie. The formerly innocent souls are now malevolent spirits who loathe the living and endeavor to spread their blight into the neighboring village and ultimately across the land unless the characters can stop them and hopefully administer some justice of their own to the callous murderers who caused their untimely deaths.

ADVENTURE SUMMARY

This adventure has several moving parts that may make it appear daunting to run at first glance. It includes red herrings and some investigative digging to unlock the mystery, which will likely consume several hours of gameplay as the characters sort through the evidence and testimony to reach their

AREA MAP
N
Maizefield
*
Village Square
Noble Houses
1 Square - 500 Feet

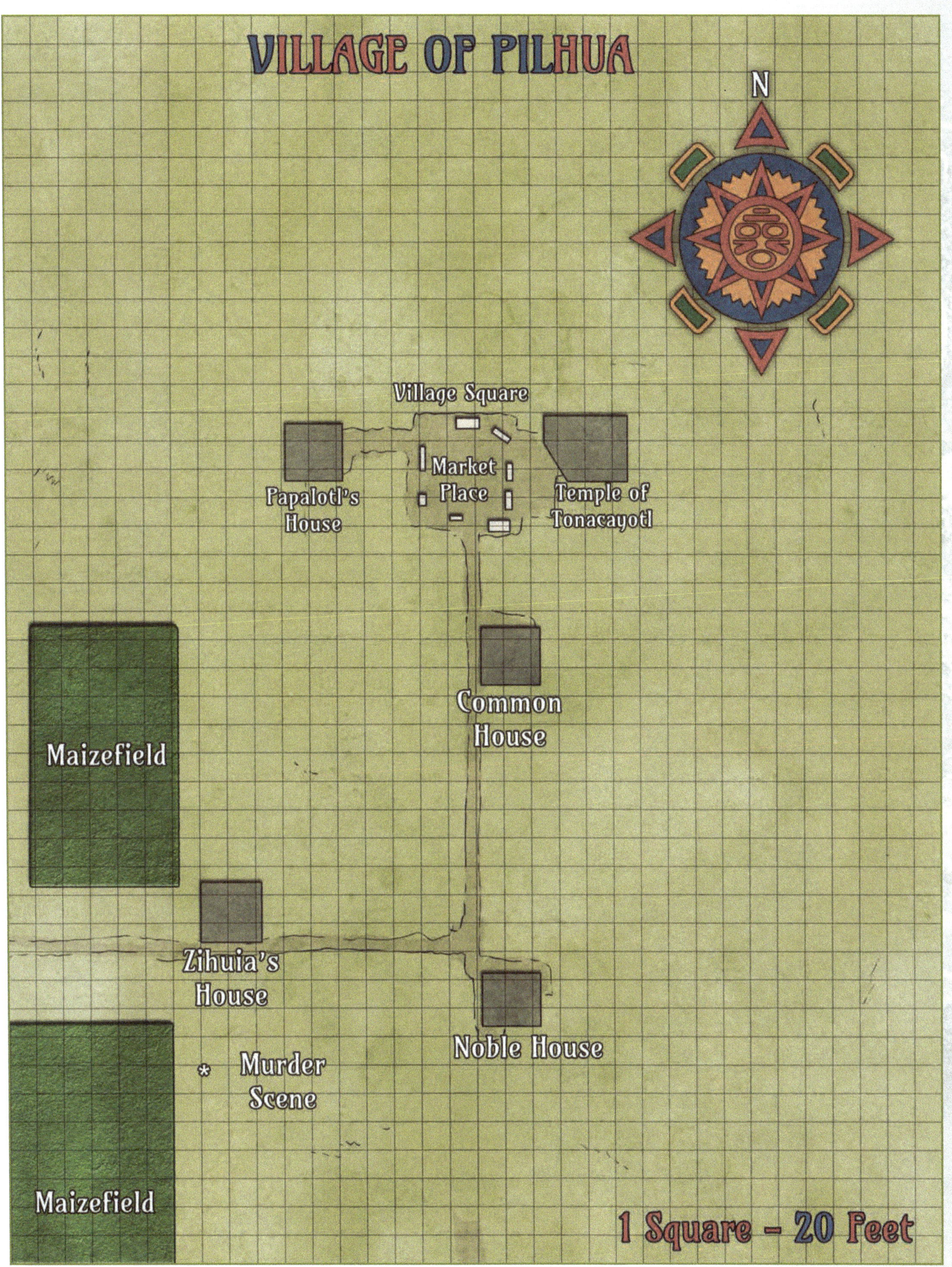

VILLAGE OF PILHUA
N
Village Square
Papalotl's House
Market Place
Temple of Tonacayotl
Common House
Maizefield
Zihuia's House
Noble House
Murder Scene
Maizefield
1 Square – 20 Feet

conclusions. Two forthcoming sections, **Places of Interest** and **People of Interest**, detail the information the adventurers can gather from those sites and individuals. To avoid confusion and to keep the adventure on track, these are the key facts in the story:

• A wahuapa (maizefolk) camouflaged itself as an ordinary maize plant in Zihuia's field and waited for an opportunity to attack and kill a random victim (Zihuia) to sow terror in the village. After the killing, the creature fled back to the manipulated maizefield outside the village.

• Zihuia and Icihua's marital and financial difficulties are just red herrings. They play no role in the murder.

• Ciahuatl, Conto's fiancée, blames the town's leader, Papalotl, for failing to find her betrothed, prompting her to direct her cacalotls to attack Papalotl and the villagers.

• Mixoch and Temilaz's other victim, Uetzopilli, emerged from the grave as a sword wight who makes his way to Pilhua to seek revenge against his murderers.

• The wahuapas plan to return to the village to take more innocent lives unless the characters stop them.

The trail of death and mayhem ultimately leads back to Conto and Chipinia's killing more than one year ago where the two unrequited horrors created an enclosed maze crafted from manipulated maize plants.

STARTING THE ADVENTURE

The characters are free to start the adventure in the village of Pilhua or while traveling through the area on their way somewhere else. Ideally the characters arrive sometime during the day or the early evening because the story's events unfold rather quickly over the course of the first evening and throughout the overnight hours. An earlier arrival allows the adventurers an opportunity to get the lay of the land and to become embroiled in the mystery gripping Pilhua rather than trying to catch up on details after the fact. Of course, if the characters make their way to the village very late in the evening, you can delay the adventure's events until the following evening and allow the characters to explore the village and gather some information before getting the tale fully underway. In every case, the adventure's opening act generally starts with the characters hearing about Zihuia's mysterious killing and investigating it.

Although the adventure is intended to be set on the island of Tehuatl, which is a new addition to the world of the Lost Lands, you can have the adventure take place in any village of your choosing with some minor adjustments.

ADVENTURE HOOKS

You may use any of the following devices to get the characters involved in the storyline shortly before or when they arrive in Pilhua.

JUSTICE NEVER DONE

It has been more than one year since their children Conto and Chipinia disappeared from their home one day and never returned. Despite an exhaustive search and the village's sympathy, the teenagers' parents, **Itoloc and Namaquia** remain determined to find their missing son and daughter. They are resolute that something untoward happened to them, but they cannot offer any evidence supporting their assertion or further leads regarding their whereabouts. When they learned about Zihuia's murder, they believe his death must have some correlation to their children's predicament as killings are extremely rare in the settlement. While gnolls and other monsters have troubled the village throughout its history, they always leave telltale hallmarks of their presence whenever they strike. Itoloc and Namaquia cannot offer any monetary reward, but they happily arrange a marriage with their surviving son **Oquimon** or priestess daughter **Nequilti** to a character who returns their children to them or discovers their true fate. See the upcoming **Speaking with the Family** sidebar for more details about the information they can provide to the characters during their interactions with them.

Itoloc and Namaquia CR 1/2
XP 200
hp 10 (Pathfinder Roleplaying Game GameMastery Guide, "Farmer")

Nequilti CR 1/2
XP 200
hp 5 (Pathfinder Roleplaying Game GameMastery Guide, "Acolyte")

Oquimon CR 1/2
XP 200
hp 9 (Appendix B: NPCs, "Tribal Warrior")

MURDER MOST FOUL

Zihuia's widow, **Icihua** has little confidence in the local authorities solving her deceased husband's murder. Icihua descends from Itztliteotl, making her one of the village's few coconeteotls (nobles) and giving her greater pull and status within Pilhua than the children's commoner parents. Despite her overt melancholy and hysteria, some wary villagers cast a suspicious eye toward the grieving widow who openly flirted with younger warriors throughout her marriage to Zihuia, who was also a nobleperson of lesser rank than his spouse. Cognizant of these chattering voices, the wealthy woman approaches the characters to investigate the matter and ultimately clear her name. Of course, she denies any involvement in his death, which is a truthful assertion, though she gets more squirrelly when asked about her professed love for her husband and the rumors about her affairs with other men. While in her late 30s, the childless Icihua remains a charming, attractive woman with considerable financial means compared to her fellow villagers. She offers the characters a personal family heirloom and a pair of turquoise earplugs worth 250 gp to primarily absolve her of any involvement in the killing, and secondarily to solve the case. If you use this hook, see the upcoming **Speaking with Icihua** sidebar for details regarding Icihua's knowledge about the crime.

Icihua CR 1/2
XP 200
hp 7 (Pathfinder Roleplaying Game NPC Codex, "Princess")

AN EXPLOSIVE SITUATION

Not all maize is created equally nor serves the same purpose. The small village of Pilhua is like many others scattered across the Caya Grasslands, but some inhabitants swear the farmers who live here grow the finest popcorn on the island and season the exploding kernels better than anyone else. Maize aficionados consider the pilgrimage to the community to be worth the effort. If you opt to use this hook, the characters themselves may be on their way to the town to partake in a popcorn festival that occurs during the 10th day of every month, or they are traveling here at the behest of someone else who sent them to purchase two bushels of popcorn from a local pochteca. In this case, the characters may visit the murderers **Mixoch and Temilaz** to conduct the legitimate transactions (see the **Speaking with Mixoch and Temilaz** sidebar). During their stay in the village, the characters ultimately learn about the killing and may be prompted to further explore the matter of their own accord or at another party's request.

Mixoch and Temilaz CR 3
XP 800
hp 22 (Appendix B: NPCs, "Mixoch and Temilaz")

Part One: The Village of Pilhua

With a population just under 300 residents, the predominately Aztli community of Pilhua is an agrarian community where its resident farmers cultivate maize along with squash, quinoa, tomatoes, chili peppers, and cilantro. The town's 271 commoners live on land they lease at a low cost from the town's 26 nobles including its seven coconeteotls and Icihua, the widow of the murder victim Zihuia who was also a noble of lesser status than his spouse. Pilhua stretches out across roughly two square miles of ground with the nobility living in furnished, multiroom homes clustered around the village's aqueducts that divert water into the community from neighboring rivers and streams, while the commoners occupy simple one-room abodes built on chinampas along Pilhua's outskirts and edges. Regardless of social status, each residence also features an attached temazcal that functions as a primitive sauna where family members can relax and also cleanse their bodies after an arduous day in the fields.

When not at home or tending to their crops, villagers gather on the grounds of the Temple of Tonacayotl where vibrant stalks of the vital plant tower almost 10 feet above the earth. Here, they exchange the news of the day while socializing with their neighbors as well as bringing offerings of maize to the deity venerated within this humble yet important religious center. **Cintecuhtli** tends to his worshippers' spiritual and earthly needs. A fellow coconeteotl in his own right, Cintecuhtli is an influential village member, though his authority rarely extends beyond matters outside his sacred purview. Instead, **Papalotl** exercises secular authority over the village. He and his contingent of 17 **jaguar warriors** keep the peace within Pilhua. Papalotl is a quichtic, a noble title earned through his bravery on the battlefield that he earned in his youth when he singlehandedly felled seven gnolls during a raid more than 30 years ago. Now approaching 50 years of age, Papalotl frequently relives the glory days of his younger days when his fighting skills were at their zenith.

Most families' roots in the village go back multiple generations with many residents being at least distantly related to each other. The human Aztlis dominate the community, with a handful of half-elf Poqozas and elves from the neighboring forest as well as several halflings and gnomes rounding out the settlement. Self-sufficient farming accounts for a substantial percentage of Pilhua's economy, with some families selling surplus yields to visiting merchants outside the Temple of Tonacayotl. However, there are 23 artisans of different races in the village who manufacture goods such as leather, adventuring gear and equipment, tools, implements, herbal remedies, artworks, and other specialty items catering to villagers and the officially licensed pochtecas who frequent the crude marketplace outside the holy site's vestibule.

Cintecuhtli	**CR 4**
XP 1,200	
hp 28 (Appendix B: NPCs, "Cintecuhtli")	
Papalotl	**CR 4**
XP 1,200	
hp 38 (Appendix B: NPCs, "Papalotl")	
Jaguar Warrior (17)	**CR 1**
XP 400	
hp 17 (Appendix B: NPCs, "Jaguar Warrior")	

Rumors

Outside of a tiny minority of newcomers in Pilhua, everyone generally knows everyone else in the community for nearly their entire lives. The close bonds ensure that information, for better or worse, travels fast across the village, though accuracy sometimes takes a back seat to the news' hasty delivery. While exploring the settlement, the characters may overhear information from locals or actively gather it. A character who succeeds on a Diplomacy check may also hear more generalized gossip from third-party sources if the character can effectively communicate with the individual and the person has some knowledge of the area. Likewise, the characters may have already gained some information about the area and its people through their personal experiences and education. Characters from the Caya Grasslands have a +2 bonus on Knowledge (History) and Knowledge (Religion) to recall details and information germane to current events in the region.

A character who succeeds on a DC 10 Knowledge (History) or Knowledge (Religion) check (character's choice) as noted below remembers something about this topic that pertains to the current situation. Likewise, a character who succeeds on a DC 10 Diplomacy check while meeting the preceding conditions may also discover any of the following facts about the area. A successful check in one of the preceding fields does not grant access to every rumor. The parenthesis at the end of each rumor indicates the applicable area of expertise required to recall the information and whether the rumor is true or not.

Table 1-1: Rumors

d8	Rumor
1–2	The Temple of Tonacayotl is the only religious building in the village and the hub of activity in Pilhua. Most people gather here to discuss news, sell their crops, and socialize when not working in the fields. (History, Religion, or Diplomacy; this rumor is true)
3	Cintecuhtli, the high priest of Tonacayotl, is a good, honest man. Many villagers revere him as a father figure. He attends to all spiritual ceremonies and rites in the settlement. (Religion, Diplomacy; this rumor is true)
4	Someone murdered a local man named Zihuia. Everyone except the authorities suspect that his wife Icihua knows more than she is saying about the killing. (Diplomacy; this rumor is true)
5	Pilhua is under the Aztli Confederation's jurisdiction, and Papalotl serves as the village's foremost secular authority. (History or Diplomacy; this rumor is true)
6	If you need any goods, Mixoch and Temilaz, the local pochtecas, are the men to see. (Diplomacy; this rumor is true)
7	The gnolls have been more active lately. An attack is imminent. (Diplomacy; this rumor is false)
8	Poqoza traders sometimes visit Pilhua to peddle illegal substances such as intoxicating mushrooms and cacti. (Diplomacy; this rumor is partly true since Uetzopilli no longer comes here)

The following tales also circulate through the village, though they are available only to a character who succeeds by 5 or more on the preceding checks and contacts someone who would reasonably possess this type of knowledge.

Table 1-2: Rumors

d8	Rumor
1–2	Two local siblings, Conto and Chipinia, vanished from the village roughly one year ago. An exhaustive search of the village and the surrounding area turned up no traces of the teenagers or their ultimate fate. (Diplomacy; this rumor is true)
3	Conto was engaged to Ciahuatl. She is bitter about the lack of progress in finding her fiancé and has grown distant and melancholy since his disappearance. (Diplomacy; this rumor is true and available only if the character already heard the preceding rumor)

4	Zihuia and Icihua had numerous problems during their marriage. Zihuia drank too much and dabbled in drugs. She is too flirtatious and has supposedly had affairs with others, though no one has ever admitted to that. (Diplomacy; this rumor is true)
5	Mixoch and Temilaz supply psychedelic substances on occasion, though they have not done so ever since Cintecuhtli spoke to them about the dangers and morality of doing so. (Diplomacy; this rumor is partly true, as the pair stopped selling drugs but not because of the high priest's interference)
6	A priest of the gnoll's god Itzcuin has infiltrated the village and is distracting the residents to pave the way for an attack. (Diplomacy; this rumor is false)

The following stories are not divulged randomly. The character must make a specific inquiry or conduct research about that topic and succeed by 10 or more on one of the preceding checks.

Maize Monsters: Spilt innocent blood can give birth to the dreaded wahuapa, the maizefolk who occasionally stalk the grasslands. These sentient plants hate all humanoid life and seek to destroy it. (History; this rumor is true)

Unrequited: When a teenager dies tragically, the soul may be reborn as an undead spirit approximately one year after their death. (Religion; this rumor is true)

POINTS OF INTEREST

The following section details important points of interest the characters find within Pilhua. The characters are free to explore the village in its entirety, though most homes and their adjoining land provide nothing of interest to solving the mystery enveloping the community.

TEMPLE OF TONACAYOTL

Although primarily designed to be a religious center, the single-story Temple of Tonacayotl proves to be multifunctional. The mud-brick structure includes an outer vestibule where worshippers and villagers gather, and an inner shrine where followers offer maize at the feet of a limestone man-sized statue of the god depicted as a young man with yellow hair. It takes a successful DC 5 Knowledge (Religion) check to identify the god of maize as the sculpture's divine subject. Smaller religious iconography dedicated to the other members of the Aztli pantheon occupy small niches built into the circular chamber's walls. These include paintings and miniature wood figurines of Yaocteotl, Itztliteotl, Zipe-Toteque, Quiahuitl, Nonotzali, and Micoateotl. It takes a successful DC 5 Knowledge (Religion) check to identify the subjects of these artworks, though any Aztli character may do so automatically without a check. While the Aztlis still provide offerings to these deities, Tonacayotl's priest Cintecuhtli performs no formal rites or ceremonies to honor them. Nonetheless, Pilhua's Aztli residents still venerate these important gods and honor them in the sanctity of their homes.

Cintecuhtli (see **Appendix B: NPCs**) also resides within the temple, dwelling in a bland room connected to the inner shrine that contains a plain, linen mat for sleeping and a small enclosed alcove for steam bathing. The middle-aged priest never married and devoted his life to praising Tonacayotl, who has blessed the village with bountiful crops throughout his 22-year tenure and serves as the village's de facto healer. Cintecuhtli uses medicinal herbs he grows in a garden on the temple grounds to remedy minor ailments and illnesses. For more serious injuries, the priest relies upon the magical powers his benefactor grants him to close wounds and to cure diseases. Despite living alone for nearly his entire adult life, Cintecuhtli is a gregarious man who enjoys the company of others. Despite holding the lesser noble title of tlahtoh for his services to the temple, the village priest frequently dines at the homes of commoners who welcome him into their humble abodes with open arms. He is renowned for his ability to shape perfectly round tortillas and his ability to flawlessly season any maize dish, which runs counter to his vanilla lifestyle choices. Because of his extensive contacts with the villagers, he is practically the fountain of all information in Pilhua.

Zihuia's recent murder greatly disturbs him. Naturally, he turned to Tonacayotl for magical guidance and received a cryptic response telling him "the sins of the present have deep roots in the past." He also cleansed Zihuia's

ZIHUIA'S CORPSE

Still clothed in his bloody cloak, the body displays eight laceration wounds across his body: one on his face, two on his back, two on his right arm, two on his right leg, and a final slice across his abdomen. A character who examines the body and succeeds on a DC 15 Heal check concludes that a sharp, serrated weapon or appendage inflicted the injuries. Likewise, a character who does the same and succeeds on a DC 20 Perception check finds tiny strands of greenish-brown, silky fibers embedded in the wounds. It takes a successful DC 5 Knowledge (Nature) check to identify them as fibers from a maize husk, which seems inexplicable as Zihuia was not found in the maizefield and had no contact with the plants. Cintecuhtli has no explanation for how the corn silk got into the wounds, as he cleaned the body with a cloth.

If the characters communicate with Zihuia's spirit through a *speak with dead* spell or similar magic, the victim communicates only what he saw. Because of his severely intoxicated state at the time of his killing, his answers are basic and vague. He recalls feeling a sharp object tear through his skin several times and makes a cryptic reference to the "damn maize stalk wrapping around him."

body before its cremation, which he plans to attend to the following morning. The temple stores the corpse in a cellar underneath the inner shrine that is accessible through a door in the floor. If the characters ask to see the body, Cintecuhtli politely declines their request. However, a character who succeeds on a Diplomacy or Intimidate check overcomes the priest's initial reluctance and causes him to grant the individual permission to examine Zihuia's lifeless body, though he still insists on maintaining proper decorum while doing so.

During any discussion about the killing, Cintecuhtli makes an offhanded remark about Conto and Chipinia. He nonchalantly tells the characters that his followers never experienced these types of crimes for most of his time here, but first it was the missing children and now a murdered villager. If the characters probe for more details, Cintecuhtli vividly recalls praying with the family and conducting extensive searches throughout the area looking for the lost siblings with no luck. He presumes they either ran away, which he highly doubts, or met a tragic end, likely at the hands of gnolls who occasionally raid outlying farms. He laments that the family still hopes to find their precious son and daughter, but he sadly believes their efforts to be in vain. He also mentions that Conto's fiancée Ciahuatl still grieves for the man she was to marry and has withdrawn into her own melancholy.

When he returns to the subject of Zihuia's death, he also expresses frustration and uncertainty. If asked for a connection between the man's killing and the children's disappearance, none readily comes to mind. The nobleman had little if any contact with the young commoners. If asked about Icihua, the grieving widow, he does not believe that she had any role in her husband's killing. Nonetheless, he reluctantly relents that her flirtatiousness could lead some to speculate she played a part in his death. However, Cintecuhtli also admits that Zihuia had plenty of flaws, including a penchant for drinking too much pulque and occasionally embarking on mind trips using psychedelics smuggled into the village from south of the Great Canal. If the characters ask him about the latter topic, he says that Zihuia had not partaken in this indulgence for at least several months, though a successful DC 15 Sense Motive check suggests there is more to the story than he initially acknowledges. If the characters press him further about the matter, he reluctantly admits that Mixoch and Temilaz, two local pochtecas, supposedly sold psychedelic mushrooms and other hallucinogens they acquired from Poqoza traders, but they seem to no longer be involved in selling these goods in the village, a fact he attributes to a conversation he had with the pair several months earlier in response to Zihuia's erratic behavior.

Finding **Mixoch and Temilaz** (see **Appendix B: NPCs**) proves easy during the day. The temple grounds serve as a meeting place for villagers and the center of commerce within the community, and the two pochtecas conduct business here throughout the day alongside farmers, artisans, and other local residents peddling their goods. The duo hustles their wares to their regular customers who venture to the temple grounds only once per week or every other week.

Venlo Innova (see **Appendix B: NPCs**) is also a mainstay in the public marketplace. The gnome inventor fashions himself as an "improver" rather than an innovator. He enhances already existing items with mixed success. Venlo lives and works out of his shop roughly one-half mile from the temple. He lugs his goods back and forth with him using a modified sled that he drags along the ground on his way to and from his home, which offers an example of one of his more productive design upgrades. Venlo also imagines

Venlo the Detective

The characters are free to use Venlo's services at their peril. Venlo theorizes Conto and Chipinia were abducted by astral travelers he believes came from one of the planet's two moons. His "proof" for this theory derives from the villagers' inability to find any physical evidence regarding their fate. He thinks only supernatural beings could accomplish such a feat. Fortunately, he has not yet formulated a solid theory about Zihuia's death, though he leans toward exploring crackpot explanations over rational ones, including the return of his imaginary astral travelers, Zihuia's supposed involvement with an agricultural cabal intent on replacing maize with amaranth, and assassins who masquerade as mice. However, if the characters inspect the murder scene and perform certain other tasks with Venlo in tow, he can provide another set of eyes and ears to examine the facts of the case while trying to steer him away from the fantastical.

himself to be an amateur investigator who once again demonstrates uneven performance. He excels at analyzing and interpreting physical evidence, yet he fails miserably at gathering testimony and interacting with others. He is prone to making outlandish accusations, even though the facts he uncovered refute his assertions, and he baselessly thinks everyone lies to him. Venlo's shortcomings aside, the gnome gladly offers to sell his adventuring gear to prospective customers as well as offer his opinions and assistance if the characters ask questions about Zihuia's killing or the missing children.

Zihuia's Home (The Murder Scene)

Although members of nobility, the home Zihuia shared with his wife Icihua seems hardly befitting for one of the village's best-known power couples. It is modestly sized even when compared to the commoners' residences, and it has hardly any amenities for people of their status. The surprisingly rundown abode's only selling point is its location. A character who visits the site and succeeds on a DC 15 Perception check takes note of the unkempt property's poor condition for people of such purported means.

Icihua found her husband's body facedown at the edge of their small farm roughly 110 feet from the door shortly before midnight. A character who succeeds on a DC 10 Perception check discovers pottery shards littering the ground between the residence and the murder location. A character who examines the pieces and succeeds on a DC 15 Knowledge (Local) check identifies the shards as part of a jar that contained pulque. However, Papalotl removed the corpse shortly after arriving on the scene. When the characters arrive here, the only evidence they find are three streaks of blood covering the soil 15 feet from the first row of maize flourishing in the fertile earth.

The plants appear ordinary from a distance. However, a character who enters into the maizefield and walks among the stalks notices a deep hole in the ground approximately 45 feet from the murder scene with a successful DC 10 Perception check. The disturbed earth is loose yet still moist. A character who examines the dirt and succeeds on a DC 15 Knowledge (Nature) check concludes the ground was excavated within the last 24 hours. Furthermore, the abscess oddly appears in a spot between two rows of maize, indicating that no one planted maize in the unearthed location. Further digging in the cavity reveals no residual roots or other fibrous plant material around the hole's edges. However, a character who succeeds on a DC 20 Survival check locates an unusual set of tracks leading from the void toward the murder scene. The visible depressions in the ground appear to be made by something fibrous or tendril-like rather than humanoid or even monstrous feet. A character who then succeeds on a DC 20 Knowledge (Nature) check surmises that some type of vine or other plant material made the impressions in the ground. While it is possible to follow the trail from the hole to the murder site, Papalotl and his warriors made footprints around where the blood splattered, making it impossible to distinguish where the presumed perpetrator went afterward.

Common House

The villagers use this lodge to accommodate visitors, though its furnishings are sparse and amenities limited. It is simply an open space with linen mats for sleeping and a steam room for bathing. If the characters opt to stay here during their visit to Pilhua, there is no cost, though it is customary to make

Speaking with Icihua

Characters who venture to Zihuia's murder site are likely to eventually meet with and speak to his widow, Icihua. Rumors constantly swirl around the noblewoman, yet contrary to these stories, she never betrayed Zihuia even though she had ample reason to do so on many occasions. If the adventurers speak to her, the vivacious woman falls back on her natural instinct to charm her attentive audience. Icihua's account of the events leading up to the murder are truthful, though she may gloss over an inconvenient fact when it suits her needs. She provides the following information without coaxing:

• Around midnight, she and Zihuia got into an argument over his excessive pulque consumption. Her husband stormed out of their home with a jar of pulque in hand.

• When he did not return within a few minutes like he usually would, she left the home to look for him. In the moonlight, she saw him lying face down on the ground. Naturally, she presumed he had passed out again, but when she drew closer to check on him, she noticed that blood had soaked his cloak.

• Gashes tore through the fabric and his flesh. She could tell he had stopped breathing and was obviously dead. Fearful that whatever harmed her husband might still be out there, she rushed to summon Papalotl for aid and to investigate the crime.

• Although he clearly died a violent death, Icihua heard nothing after Zihuia left and before she discovered the body.

• She and her husband own the land, which they lease to multiple commoner families who live on the village's outskirts. They collect a percentage of their crop yields, which they use to feed themselves and also to sell for additional income. To the best of her knowledge, no one has been in the maizefield for several days because of the persistent rain.

Icihua readily volunteers the preceding information, but she intentionally withholds the following details from the characters. Engaging in one of the following lines of questioning requires the character to already possess some facts pertaining to the subject matter and to succeed on a Diplomacy or Intimidate check.

Financial Problems: Icihua acknowledges that her husband squandered his money on pulque, hallucinogens, and fly-by-night schemes. A few times, he came close to risking his noble status because of his misfortune, but they always paid his creditors in the end.

Drug Use: Icihua admits Zihuia used psychedelic substances on some occasions, but says he had not done so for at least the past several months. If pressed about where he obtained the hallucinogens, she believes Mixoch and Temilaz sold them to him, but he never specifically told her where he purchased them.

Maizefield Hole: Icihua knows nothing about the anomalous hole in the maizefield. She swears they planted their seeds in perfect rows. She never saw any strange activity there.

Her Indiscretions: Icihua vehemently denies any allegations about her infidelity. She begrudgingly confesses to sometimes being too flirtatious toward her male and even female admirers, though her relationships never went beyond friendship or playful banter.

Possible Suspects: She swears no one had any reason to harm her husband. He had settled his debts and no longer partook in drug use. Excessive pulque consumption was his worst problem, and no one would kill him over drinking too much.

an offering to the Temple of Tonacayotl for its hospitality in maintaining and cleaning the facility. Guests are also expected to keep the common house tidy and exhibit proper etiquette while staying in the equivalent of someone else's home. Although there are no other visitors at the time, farmhands and nobles occasionally wander in to gather some news about the world outside of Pilhua.

People of Interest

The preceding section describes the characters' interactions with Cintecuhtli, the high priest of Tonacayotl, Venlo Innova the gnome inventor, and Icihua, the grieving widow. However, the characters are likely to want to speak with other individuals in town while conducting their investigation. The following paragraphs describe their interactions with other residents who can shed some light on the events plaguing Pilhua as well as some directly responsible for setting the tragic chain of events into motion.

Speaking with the Family

Itoloc and Namaquia readily volunteer everything they know about that fateful day without coaxing.

• Conto and Chipinia were extremely close and frequently traveled together throughout the village and sometimes beyond it. Nonetheless, they always came home safe afterward.

• No one recalls seeing them that day, which is unusual because they knew everyone and would frequently encounter someone during the course of their travels.

• They never said where they were going that day.

• Conto never would have left of his own accord. He deeply loved his fiancée Ciahuatl and looked forward to marrying her in the coming days.

• Gnolls have periodically attacked the village or raided outlying farms, but there were no other reports of their activity in the days before or following their disappearance.

Nequilti and her sister, who was 16 months older, did not have the same tight bond as her two older siblings. However, the pair sometimes confided in their older brother Omiquin. Despite his concern for his missing siblings, he is a little more tightlipped than his parents. It takes a successful DC 15 Sense Motive check to recognize that he is not as forthright as everyone else when discussing the matter with the rest of the family. Pressing him for further details requires the character to succeed on a Diplomacy or Intimidate check. On a success, Omiquin asks the character to step outside his parents' earshot to convey his additional information:

• His younger brother and sister liked to smoke tobacco and drink pulque he acquired for them on occasion. They frequently went to one of several isolated areas outside village, but he showed Papalotl the places he knew about, and they found nothing.

• For a short while, the trio partook in ingesting peyote and psychedelic mushrooms. Omiquin stopped using them shortly after his siblings' disappearance.

• Ciahuatl took his brother's death very hard. She rarely if ever speaks to anyone unless forced to do so and endlessly obsesses over tragedies.

If the characters further question him about the narcotic substance use, it takes an additional successful Diplomacy or Intimidate check at a -5 penalty to pry the final piece of information from the protective oldest brothers:

• Omiquin purchased the substances from Mixoch and Temilaz, whom he believed acquired them from a pochteca trader. However, they stopped selling the illicit goods roughly one year ago. They never gave an explanation as to why other than vague hints about having a problem with their supplier.

• Although Omiquin primarily interacted with the pochtecas, his younger brother and sister were at least slightly familiar with them.

Conto and Chipinia's Family

Characters who learn of the siblings' disappearance one year earlier may wish to speak with their family to learn more about the teenagers and to get some additional insight from them about their suspected fate. If you used the **Justice Never Done** hook, the characters may acquire this information from the family members at the adventure's onset. The children's father Itoloc and mother Namaquia still mourn the presumed loss of their middle son and daughter. Their older son Omiquin and younger daughter Nequilti also suffer on a daily basis though they are more resilient than their aging and obviously devastated parents. The family gladly welcomes anyone willing to uncover what really happened to their missing children.

Speaking with the Farmhands

Although not intentionally evasive, Nitla and Alihui are reluctant to speak ill of the nobles who own the land they lease. However, when questioned about the following subjects, they provide these answers without coaxing:

• *Zihuia/Icihua:* They and their family have worked for the couple since shortly after they married and acquired the land. The couple has problems from time to time, but so does everyone else.

• *Hole/Abscess:* The farmhands swear every row of maize was planted in straight lines. No one recalls ever seeing a cavity in the ground on the property or can explain how it got there.

A character must succeed on a Diplomacy or Intimidate check to gain the following information from the farmhands' leader regarding these subjects:

• *Zihuia's Lifestyle:* Zihuia occasionally dabbled in taking hallucinogens, but his main issue was his excessive pulque consumption. He and Icihua frequently argued about his alcoholism. However, when he was sober, which was less often than when he was drunk, Zihuia was an industrious and kind person.

• *Icihua's Lifestyle:* Despite the stories circulating within the village and her vivacious personality, Icihua remained faithful to her husband throughout their marriage. She certainly tired of Zihuia's vices, but she loved him nonetheless.

• *Financial Issues:* Zihuia's debts almost got the better of them, but they almost wriggled their way out of a tight spot and satisfied their creditors in the end.

Farmhands

Characters who meet with Icihua may wish to speak with the men and women who plant, till, and harvest the crops from her maizefield. In all, 14 adults work on Icihua's land, but the junior farmhands defer all questions to the team's de facto leaders **Nitla and Alihui**. The husband and wife team have worked for Zihuia and Icihua for 15 years along with their younger siblings, children, and extended family. They live in a small home on the village's outskirts roughly one-half mile from Zihuia's home.

Nitla and Alihui   CR 1/2
XP 200
hp 10 (Pathfinder Roleplaying Game GameMastery Guide, "Farmer")

Papalotl

The noble warrior Papalotl interacts with the Aztli Confederation's delegation from Ixtla and also wields secular authority on the alliance's behalf over Pilhua, though he is not an official member or representative of Ixtla or the confederation. Papalotl earned his stripes and well-earned reputation on the battlefield during his skirmishes against gnoll raiders and the occasional monster that plagued the village. He prefers fighting an obvious enemy he can see and has little interest or talent for unraveling mysteries. When he arrived at the scene of the crime, Papalotl was more interested in tracking down the perpetrator through military means rather than gathering evidence and unmasking the culprit. Because he and his soldiers so badly trampled down the area around Zihuia's body, even the recent spate of rain could not preserve any tracks or trail leading away from the crime scene.

Papalotl becomes very defensive if the characters question his investigative skills or his actions. In that case, he terminates the conversation with them and refuses to answer any additional questions. If the characters persist, he ultimately threatens to arrest them and turn them over to the authorities in Ixtla for a stay in the peticalli (Aztli penitentiary). The warriors under his command cannot provide any additional information beyond what Papalotl already provided.

SPEAKING WITH CIAHUATL

Characters who meet Ciahuatl encounter an aloof, distant young woman obsessed with finding her missing lover and avenging him if something untoward happened to him. She speaks as little as possible and frequently makes facial expressions and gestures indicating her clear disinterest in helping the heroes. While her justifiable fury led her down a vile path, she is not wholly irredeemable. When portraying Ciahuatl during her meeting with the characters, it is important to remember that she is still not an adult and has never committed a truly evil act during her short lifetime. Her dejection and lack of trust in the abilities of others has basis in fact. Getting through her tough exterior and appealing to her remaining vestiges of humanity poses a significant challenge to the characters.

Getting her to say anything at all requires a successful Bluff, Diplomacy, or Intimidate check and even then, she only offers the following vague details with a detached attitude:

• Conto and his younger sister disappeared a little more than one year ago.

• The villagers went looking for them, but could not find them. Then again, Papalotl and his soldiers could not find a jaguar in an empty room.

• She was deeply in love with Conto and was committed to spending the rest of her life with him and having a family.

• No one else will ever make her happy.

Getting any additional information beyond these cursory items proves exceptionally difficult as the haughty teenager ignores the strangers and declines to answer any more questions, claiming she has nothing further to say about the matter. She reverts to staring blankly into space and softly singing lullabies to assuage her anguish and to reinforce her unwillingness to continue the conversation with the characters. Bullying, belittling, or lying to her are ineffective tactics and only further her resolve not to cooperate. If the characters resort to these methods, she grows tired of their presence and demands that they leave her sight at once.

Characters who refuse are in for a rude awakening as the clever Ciahuatl escorts the characters out of her home and discreetly signals for the 10 **cacalotls** hiding in the maizefield outside her home to attack the characters after they leave the residence. The monsters behave as described in the **Murder of Cacalotls** section, though in this instance, Ciahuatl stays out of the fray, leaving the constructs to fend for themselves while feigning having no pre-existing relationship with the monsters. Of course, convincing the characters of her innocence if they survive the rendezvous with the cacalotls requires her to succeed on a Bluff check. If the characters leave of their own accord, the cacalotls remain silent and continue to hide in the field.

Cacalotl (10)   CR 3
XP 800
hp 31 (Appendix A: New Monsters, "Cacalotl")

A character who wants additional information from Ciahuatl must succeed on a Bluff, Diplomacy, or Intimidate check with a -5 penalty. However, if a character identifies Mixoch and Temilaz as her fiancé's killer and can offer at least a scintilla of proof, the situation reverses itself. The character has a +5 bonus on this check instead. You may also reward a character by allowing the character to make the check without penalty if the individual acknowledges Ciahuatl's passionate feelings for Conto and makes a direct appeal to these powerful emotions. The young woman is not irreparably evil, at least not yet, and can be swayed from her current course of action with the proper coaxing. In this case, Ciahuatl breaks down and tells the characters the following information:

• She suspects someone murdered Conto and Chipinia and that their deaths played a central role in the formation of an enclosed maizefield outside the village. The exact link eludes her, but she knows the wahuapas (maizefolk) guard the entrance to the complex.

• Spilt humanoid blood creates wahuapas, and at least one of these creatures is responsible for killing Zihuia. She believes the monsters started hunting her down after she traveled to the manipulated maizefield several days earlier.

• Conto's older brother Omiquin sometimes gave his younger brother and sister pulque, tobacco, and occasionally other hallucinogens that he acquired from an unknown source. The pair would occasionally ingest and smoke in secluded locales outside the village.

SPEAKING WITH PAPALOTL

Papalotl has no love for words or speaking with others, but if the characters interview him about the murder or the children's disappearance, the gruff soldier first asks about their authority to pose such questions to him. It takes a successful Bluff, Diplomacy, or Intimidate check to get past his first line of defense. On a successful check, Papalotl reveals the following details about the evening of Zihuia's murder:

• Icihua summoned Papalotl and his troops to her home after discovering Zihuia's body outside their home several minutes earlier. When he and his subordinates examined the body, they noticed lacerations that tore through his clothing and sliced through his skin, killing him.

• He and his soldiers fanned out throughout the area but could find no physical evidence that would lead to a potential suspect or a trail.

• Everyone knew Zihuia and Icihua had issues, but he understood they were working through their issues. Icihua told him that Zihuia left the house after an argument and that she heard nothing until she found his body. Icihua appeared genuinely shocked and saddened by her husband's untimely demise.

• He and his soldiers took Zihuia's body to the Temple of Tonacayotl for funerary rights.

CIAHUATL

Conto's grieving fiancée may be only 16 years of age, but her youth cannot comfort her pain. She deeply mourns the loss of her prospective future husband. The melancholy teenager also seethes that she and his family never received justice. **Ciahuatl** (see **Appendix B: NPCs**) expresses her sorrow and anger by refusing to wash her face, wear jewelry, or tend to her luxurious hair, which has grown tangled and unmanageable. She eats just enough to survive and spends nearly all her time in a secluded enclave several hundred feet beyond her family's maizefield communing with the cihuateteo. Her parents **Otla and Coyani** are at a loss to help their distraught daughter rebuild her shattered life.

The aloof young woman blames Papalotl's ineptitude and the villagers' lack of determination and ingenuity for failing to locate Conto and his missing sister. In her darkest hours, she struck a bargain with the cihuateteo to grant her the power to succeed where all others have failed. During her travels, she located the manipulated maizefield outside the village, though she could not get past the wahuapas guarding it to further investigate the site. She believes it holds the secret to unraveling the mystery of Conto and Chipinia's fate, but the wahuapas' attack last night convinced her that they are searching for her, which forced her to spring into action earlier than she hoped as described in the **Murder of Cacalotls** section.

Otla and Coyani   CR 1/2
XP 200
hp 10 (Pathfinder Roleplaying Game GameMastery Guide,
    "Farmer")

If the characters win over Ciahuatl, she agrees to lead them to the maizefield complex and help them infiltrate it, though that is as far as she goes under that circumstance. On the other hand, characters who antagonize or fail to garner her support suffer her full wrath as described in the **Murder of Cacalotls** section. Ciahuatl's personal treasure is also described under that section.

MIXOCH AND TEMILAZ

The local pochtecas have been in the community for six years and have earned a reputation for being hard negotiators who can acquire exotic and illicit goods from their sources across the island. They are in their early 40s and pass themselves off as sophisticated world travelers, wearing fancy clothing and speaking with a regal demeanor. **Mixoch** and **Temilaz** (see **Appendix B: NPCs**) may be held in high esteem for their business acumen, but the content of their character leaves much to be desired. The pair occasionally robs travelers passing through areas outside of town and have been implicated in several burglaries outside of Pilhua. Rumors of their involvement in these activities cast a cloud of suspicion over the tightknit duo who are rarely separated. Their interactions with the unreliable Poqoza merchant Uetzopilli set the adventure's events into motion when Conto and Chipinia witnessed them murder Uetzopilli, which unfortunately was not the only killing they have committed during their lengthy entrepreneurial and criminal careers.

SPEAKING WITH MIXOCH AND TEMILAZ

The gregarious pochtecas converse at breakneck speed reminiscent of a carnival barker or auctioneer trying to close a deal or drive up the price of a worthless item. Despite their rapid-fire approach, the two keep a wary eye and ear open for potentially problematic subjects and poseurs trying to pry information out of them under the guise of partaking in a business transaction. Their experience and guile have kept them alive and out of the peticalli throughout their 40 years in this world. Zihuia's recent murder heightened their defenses as they expect someone to accuse them of the killing. They suspect someone may link them to occasionally providing psychedelic drugs to Zihuia and try to pin the murder on them because of their illicit business dealings. Throughout their conversation with the characters, Mixoch and Temilaz keep their guard up, making Sense Motive checks with frequent regularity to determine if the heroes are lying to them and to gauge their true motives for meeting with them. If the conversation steers toward topics they would prefer not to discuss, such as their dealings with Zihuia and the children's disappearance, they smugly stop talking and tell the busybodies to get lost.

Under no circumstances do they confess to killing Conto, Chipinia, or Uetzopilli unless magically compelled to do so. They deflect any questions about partaking in robberies or burglaries in other areas by citing that they cannot stop people from fabricating these stories. Yet they never specifically address the allegations by deflecting these questions with curt responses. However, a character who succeeds on a Bluff, Diplomacy, or Intimidate check with a -5 penalty extracts the following answers to these specific lines of inquiry. They never willingly volunteer information to the characters:

Zihuia: They admit selling him psychedelic mushrooms and other hallucinogens on occasion, but have had no interactions with him for at least six months. He paid them in full for their products.

Omiquin: The pair claim Conto and Chipinia's older brother frequently sought them out for hallucinogenic herbs, tobacco, and pulque, which they provided until they ran out of hallucinogens about nine months ago.

Conto/Chipinia: They carefully say they had no dealings with Omiquin's younger siblings, which is a truthful statement. However, the pochtecas soft-soap their knowledge of them by saying they vaguely recall seeing them from time to time. A character can see through this lie with a successful Sense Motive check.

Drugs/Uetzopilli: A pochteca trader would sporadically supply them with psychedelics and hallucinogens, but they have not seen him for quite some time. If questioned about Uetzopilli after his re-emergence as a sword wight, Mixoch clams up, but Temilaz appears distressed about his reappearance, a fact a character can discern with a successful Sense Motive check.

Mixoch and Temilaz spend the majority of their day selling their wares in the marketplace outside the previously described **Temple of Tonacayotl**. The grifters have no personal residence and usually spend their nights at the **Common House**, the homes of noblepersons who conduct business with them, or sometimes they set up a makeshift camp just a stone's throw from their crude stand. Always on the hunt for new customers or suppliers, the two pochtecas happily engage strangers who may be interested in either avenue of business.

Characters who resort to magical means to gain information from Mixoch and Temilaz through spells and magical effects such as *detect thoughts* and *zone of truth* may learn of the pair's involvement in the murders more than one year earlier and may also receive vague references to the location where the killings took place or the motives behind them. When faced with a direct accusation, the duo spring into action to silence anyone asking about these matters. They fight as a team, maneuvering into positions to grant them sneak attacks against the characters. If faced with imminent defeat, Temilaz reluctantly surrenders while Mixoch fights to the bitter end. It still takes a successful check as previously described to exact information from him, but in this case there is no penalty. Furthermore, he admits to their role in Conto and Chipinia's deaths as well as Uetzopilli's demise. Temilaz steadfastly denies any part in Zihuia's murder and has no knowledge about that tragic crime.

Treasure: Mixoch has a leather pouch on his person that contains six pearls worth 100 gp each, a bag containing seven *+1 sling stones* along with 36 gp, and a *potion of calm animal*. Temilaz carries a pouch containing 68 gp and wears *goggles of night*.

Part Two:
Evil Descends on Pilhua

After the characters spend the first portion of the adventure gathering information and conducting their investigation in Pilhua, events kick into overdrive as the cacalotls, sword wight, and wahuapas all descend upon the village in rapid succession. Different leaders and motives guide these monsters in their actions, which ultimately forces the characters to decide how to triage the unexpected outbreak and get to the bottom of the mystery. Pilhua does not have an inn or tavern in the traditional sense and instead accommodates visitors in the **Common House** described in **Part One** of the adventure. The sequence of events unfolds in the following order: **Murder of Cacalotls**, **Wight Night**, and **Purple Maize**. After these three activities take place (or two if the characters circumvented the **Murder of Cacalotls** as explained in the preceding **Ciahuatl** section), the adventure's focus shifts to the maizefield, which is the ultimate source of the ills plaguing Pilhua. You are free to determine the exact timing of the preceding encounters, though it is suggested to give the characters enough time to recoup and heal before another enemy descends upon Pilhua and points the heroes in the direction of the maizefield.

Murder of Cacalotls

Frustrated and angry about the lack of progress in solving the missing teenagers' disappearance, Conto's fiancée **Ciahuatl** unleashes her band of 10 **cacalotls** upon the person whose futility has led her to this decision: Papalotl. Shortly after nightfall, the constructs leave their posts in the fields and coalesce around their leader Ciahuatl, who directs the monsters toward the Temple of Tonacayotl to punish the people of Pilhua for their inaction and ineptitude in locating her lost lover. When the cacalotls first appear in the village, read or paraphrase the following description:

> The pale moonlight reveals the terrifying silhouettes of 10 shambling monstrosities crafted from cloth and straw that bear sharp claws at the tips of their scrawny, fibrous fingers. The creatures fan out across the village in an apparent search for something or someone. A young woman wearing a black skirt and blouse trails behind them.

A character who already met Ciahuatl can identify her as the woman trailing behind the cacalotls with a successful DC 10 Perception check. Otherwise, the woman's identity remains unknown. Conto's distraught widow targets Papalotl whom she presumes is somewhere near the Temple of Tonacayotl where the nobles live and socialize. When the cacalotls arrive on the scene, **Papalotl** and 4 **jaguar warriors** stand ready to meet them. If Cintecuhtli, the priest of Tonacayotl, is nearby, he sees his role as tending to the injured and does not join the combat.

To simplify this encounter, Papalotl and the warriors under his command square off against five cacalotls and Ciahuatl, leaving the characters to deal with the remaining five cacalotls. Each round, the cacalotls and Ciahuatl kill one jaguar warrior, while Papalotl and the jaguar warriors slay one cacalotl every other round. Therefore, two jaguar warriors fall for every cacalotl slain by Papalotl and his underlings. Ideally, Ciahuatl keeps Papalotl and his warriors at a distance using her spells to pepper him from afar while using her cacalotls to run interference for her. Throughout the battle, the unhinged Ciahuatl bitterly complains about Papalotl's incompetence, screaming that he could not locate a priest in a temple or an ear of maize in a maizefield.

She repeatedly screams, "Where is my Conto? Where is my Conto?" Her irrational ranting borders on being delusional as her valid criticisms quickly devolve into blaming him for the sun setting in the evening and the rains not falling on command. In the span of a few minutes, the distraught young woman heaps an entire year of repressed emotions and grievances on the man she holds responsible for not taking enough action to find her beloved Conto

and his younger sister. You may choose to simulate the actual battle between Papalotl and Ciahuatl or just presume that one spell hits him each round and force him to make a saving throw against one of her magical effects, while his attacks hit her each round if he gets close enough to her to make a melee attack against her.

If the characters intervene in her plans for revenge, they can attempt to verbally convince her to call off her assault as described in the **Speaking with Ciahuatl** sidebar found in **Part One**, though doing so at this late juncture grants Ciahuatl a +5 on her checks. Despite focusing her attention on Papalotl, she retaliates against a character who attacks her. She can redirect one of her spells toward that individual or command more of her cacalotls to gang up on that person. Ciahuatl never surrenders unless a character successfully convinces her otherwise as discussed in the **Speaking with Ciahuatl** sidebar and only provides information to the characters that appears in that section. If someone kills her, she passionately proclaims her joy at being reunited with her true love and her loathing for the people who failed them during their abbreviated lives.

Cacalotl (10)   **CR 3**
XP 800
hp 31 (Appendix A: New Monsters, "Cacalotl")

Ciahuatl   **CR 4**
XP 1,200
hp 14 (Appendix B: NPCs, "Ciahuatl")

Cintecuhtli   **CR 4**
XP 1,200
hp 28 (Appendix B: NPCs, "Cintecuhtli")

Papalotl   **CR 4**
XP 1,200
hp 38 (Appendix B: NPCs, "Papalotl")

Jaguar Warrior (4)   **CR 1**
XP 400
hp 17 (Appendix B: NPCs, "Jaguar Warrior")

Treasure: Ciahuatl has two *potions of cure light wounds* in her possession, a vial of *balché**, an application of *copal glue**, a vial of *iyollo**, and a pouch of animal bones worth 2 gp.
- See **Appendix C: New Magic and Items**

Wight Night

Shortly after the tumult of the cacalotl attacks dies down, or if the characters successfully convinced Ciahuatl not to attack Pilhua, the next vengeful act gets its turn on the stage. If the characters decided to spend the night at the **Common House**, **Mixoch and Temilaz** also made the same choice this evening, bringing the characters directly into the action. Alternatively, the pair may be spending the night at a nearby nobleperson's home when another frightening cry rings through the village. The sword wight commences its hunt for his killers at the **Common House** where Uetzopilli most commonly encountered them during the overnight hours. In response to the evening's earlier activities, Papalotl, if he survived, posts 2 **jaguar warriors** as sentries to prevent further attacks. Unfortunately, 1d3 hours later, his worst fears come true when **Uetzopilli** returns to Pilhua as a sword wight accompanied by 8 **gnoll zombies** under his command. The preceding numbers presume Mixoch and Temilaz are present when the wight and his entourage arrive. If they are not, halve the number of zombies in the sword wight's company. When Uetzopilli and his gang arrive in the village, read or paraphrase the following description:

If Mixoch and Temilaz are present when the undead attack, the enraged sword wight points at the pair and wryly smiles while twirling the macuahuitl in its bony hands. It screams, "Remember me? You dumped me in that wretched hole, but here I am again. Say hello, boys, for I am only the messenger. Wait until you see what else awaits this disgusting village!"

A character who looks at the pochtecas and succeeds on a DC 5 Sense Motive check notices that they obviously recognize the undead monstrosity and appear very worried. The murderers naturally turn to their newfound "allies" for help and beg them to stop the undead horror they claim they first encountered rising from its grave several months ago. Of course, the sword wight refuses to let this lie go unchallenged and promptly refutes the pair's claim and insists that they also killed the missing children. Uetzopilli insists that they can see for themselves with a trip to the maizefield north-northwest of Pilhua.

The characters are free to let Uetzopilli and his zombies exact their revenge against the pair, but the sword wight and his minions turn their attention to the heroes when they finish with their original targets. If the adventurers intervene, Uetzopilli and four zombies attack Mixoch and Temilaz, while the remaining four zombies fight against the characters. To quickly simulate the battle between the sword wight and Mixoch and Temilaz, presume that Uetzopilli deals 9 damage each round to one of the pair and each zombie deals 3 damage per round to either target. The undead first surround Mixoch and then turns their attention to Temilaz. Each pochteca deals 10 damage each round to a zombie or 5 damage to the sword wight if they are flanking. The jaguar warriors also jump into the fray, though they only attack the zombies who deal the same damage to them, while they deal 5 damage to the zombies each round. Naturally, Uetzopilli shows no mercy to his killers, swinging at them until he and his minions savagely butcher them. You should resolve any attacks the characters make against the sword wight and the zombies in normal fashion and vice versa even if using this quick simulation method.

Gnoll Zombie (8)   **CR 1**
XP 400
hp 17 (Appendix A: New Monsters, "Zombie, Gnoll")

Jaguar Warrior (2)   **CR 1**
XP 400
hp 17 (Appendix B: NPCs, "Jaguar Warrior")

Mixoch and Temilaz   **CR 3**
XP 800
hp 22 (Appendix B: NPCs, "Mixoch and Temilaz")

Uetzopilli   **CR 6**
XP 2,400
hp 60 (Tome of Horrors 4, "Wight, Sword")

If Mixoch and Temilaz survive their close call with the sword wight, they steadfastly deny Uetzopilli's allegations, though the roles are now reversed. The characters have a +5 bonus on Bluff, Diplomacy, and Intimidate checks to extract the whole truth from them about the earlier killings and the original crime scene in the maizefield. For more details about interacting with the pochtecas, refer to the **Speaking with Mixoch and Temilaz** sidebar.

The sword wight and his zombie minions left a trail leading from the maizefield into the village. It takes a successful DC 15 Survival check to retrace the footsteps to their origin in the maizefield.

Purple Maize

After the two initial encounters within the village, the action shifts outside the village proper and into the outskirts where the characters run across the culprit responsible for Zihuia's murder. The characters by now have several potential clues that point them in that direction, including obtaining information and a confession from Mixoch and Temilaz, accompanying Ciahuatl to the maizefield, following up on Uetzopilli's statements about the maizefield, or following the trail the sword wight and his minions left back to their origin. If the characters still appear stuck on where to go next, you can use Cintecuhtli to tend to their injuries and also provide some additional insight he gained about the evils plaguing the village from divination magic. This additional insight may directly point the characters in the maizefield's direction or provide a more roundabout means of getting them there. If Venlo is tagging along with the characters, he may also serve as an informational resource for them.

Travel through the village requires the heroes to traverse the maizefields and farms scattered across the settlement's breadth. While traipsing through this landscape of towering maize interspersed with wild grasses and cereal grains, the heroes come upon 2 **wahuapas** concealed among the ordinary maize plants. It takes a successful DC 20 Knowledge (Nature) or Survival check to spot the monsters, which benefit from change foliage. When the characters move within striking range of the creatures, read or paraphrase the following description:

The monsters are incapable of speech or profound tactics. They wade into combat swinging their sharpened leaves like scythes mowing through rows of wheat. If they react before the characters close the gap between themselves and the wahuapas, one monster uses its blinding bloom to slow down the adventurers presumably rushing toward them. Otherwise, the creatures fight until destroyed, ultimately clearing the adventurers' path to the maizefield. The wahuapas may be sentient, but their intellects are child-like. If the characters can magically communicate with them, the monsters are limited to conveying simple concepts, though the plant that killed Zihuia acknowledges committing the crime in basic terms. A character who searches the nearby area and succeeds on a DC 5 Perception check discovers two holes in the ground identical to those found in the maizefield outside of Zihuia's house, thus confirming the wahuapa occupied the spot before the killing. A successful DC 10 Survival check discovers a trail leading from this location back to the maizefield. The monsters have no treasure or personal belongings.

Wahuapa (2)   **CR 4**
XP 1,200
hp 37 (Fields of Blood, "Wahuapa")

PART THREE: THE HAUNTED MAIZEFIELD

Roughly 1–1/2 miles north-northwest of Pilhua stands the maizefield, the malevolent creation of Conto and Chipinia who now haunt the dreaded maze as a pair of unrequiteds, a melancholy brood of incorporeal undead. The vengeful creatures contorted the maize plants surrounding their makeshift grave into a solid yet not impenetrable barrier of fibrous plant materials. Despite its unnatural, magical manipulation, the plants are still alive and resistant to flames if the heroes try to burn the siblings' strange creation to the ground. Inside its walls, the teenagers shaped their lair into a confounding maze replete with dead-ends and trapped passageways to ensnare trespassers and amuse the wicked duo. When the characters get within visual range of the locale, read or paraphrase the following description:

If not for its baleful origins, the haunted maizefield would be a wondrous diversion from life's drudgeries. The roughly circular, enclosed wall of maize resembles the shape of a modern-day circus big top as the husks, stalks, and leaves intertwine to form a barrier that blocks line of sight. Its walls are five feet thick and reach a height of 10 feet. The structure's roof reaches an apex of 15 feet at its center and tapers off to 10 feet along the edges, though it is only two feet thick. The characters can move through the wall, though it is difficult terrain and movement is done at 1/4 speed. The maize wall is an object that can be damaged and thus breached. It has hardness 5 and 50 hit points per 10-foot section (20 hit points for the roof) and has DR 5 / slashing. Reducing a 10-foot section of maize to 0 hit points destroys it, though the maize complex retains its structural integrity.

MAIZEFIELD FEATURES

The interior of the maizefield has similar dimensions to its exterior though, like the ceiling, the walls are only two feet thick rather than five feet thick, thus requiring only 20 damage to breach an interior wall. The ceiling is 10 feet high along the outer edges and then 1d4 + 10 feet high inside the outermost concentric ring. Unless the characters create a breach in the ceiling or outer walls, no light penetrates inside the maze, shrouding the interior in darkness. The absence of light prohibits the growth of any grasses or other vegetation between the maize rows that grow from the ground to the roof. A character who looks for tracks and succeeds on a DC 15 Survival check finds only sporadic humanoid footprints mostly in the outermost concentric rings. The inner rings seem curiously devoid of any noteworthy impressions in the ground.

The menagerie of creatures inhabiting the maze are not confined to one location, with the exception of the monsters in areas **M5** and **M6**. The siblings' spirits exert control only over the wahuapas and limited mastery over the tear collector. The remaining denizens are generally free-willed and move through the maze unimpeded, though they tend to stay away from the preceding locations. They fail to coordinate any organized response to intruders, with every inhabitant fending for itself unless an opportunity to feed or kill another creature falls into its lap. For every five minutes spent inside the maze, there is a 50% chance of one of the following encounters occurring. The randomly encountered monsters are also found in a keyed location within the maze. You should subtract any monsters the characters face here from those listed in the detailed area.

TABLE 1–3: MAZE RANDOM ENCOUNTERS

d6	Encounter
1	1d3 **bilwises** (see **Area M2**)
2	1d4 **ghouls** (see **Area M1**)
3	1 **raggedy man** (see **Area M4**)
4–6	**Vision** (see below)

VISION

A random character must succeed on a DC 14 Will saving throw or become unconscious while momentarily experiencing a horrifying vision that lasts for 1d4 rounds. Consult **Table 1–4** below to determine what the character hears and sees during this re-enactment. A character cannot experience the same vision twice.

TABLE 1–4: VISIONS WITHIN THE MAZE

d4	Vision Experienced
1	**Prelude:** A teenage boy and girl lie in a field looking up at the sky while smoking tobacco and drinking pulque. A loud commotion ensues somewhere in the distance, causing the children to get up and quietly creep through the maize to investigate it.
2	**Crime:** A teenage boy and girl hide behind maize stalks, intently watching two men and a half-elf argue about an undetermined subject. The half-elf falls to his knees and grovels as the two men plunge their tecpatls into his chest and slice his throat. The teenage boy and girl loudly scream, drawing the men's attention to them. A character who experiences this vision and succeeds on a DC 10 Perception check identifies the killers as Mixoch and Temilaz, provided the individual already met them during the course of the adventure.
3	**Murder:** Two men race toward a teenage boy and girl, who momentarily freeze. The men jump on top of them, stabbing them mercilessly with their tecpatls and slicing their throats as they helplessly scream. The teenagers fall to the ground limp, though one of the culprits broke his tecpatl blade. A character who experiences this vision and succeeds on a DC 10 Perception check identifies the killers as Mixoch and Temilaz, provided the individual already met them during the course of the adventure. That person also recognizes Mixoch as the person who broke his tecpatl.
4	**Aftermath:** Two men dump the bodies of a slain half-elf, a teenage boy, and a teenage girl into a pit in the middle of a remote maizefield. They hurriedly fill the hole with earth and transplant a maize plant on top of the crude grave to further conceal its location. A character who experiences this vision and succeeds on a DC 10 Perception check identifies the men digging the hole as Mixoch and Temilaz, provided the individual already met them during the course of the adventure.

AREA T: TRAPS

In addition to the malevolent denizens who prowl the maze, the siblings' corporeal minions also created devious mechanical devices to ensnare the unwary. Four of them are scattered throughout the complex as shown on the accompanying map. The type of trap is not designated on the map, and you are free to use any of the following traps or a combination of them.

THE HAUNTED MAIZEFIELD
T
M3
W
W
T
M2
M5
M4
M6
W
W
T
M1
W
T
N
1 Square – 10 Feet

Popcorn Trap

A pressure plate in the ground at the spot marked "T" pressurizes hardened kernels of popcorn hidden within faux husks interspersed among the neighboring maize stalks. A creature who weighs more than 50 pounds that steps on the pressure plate triggers the trap.

When the trap is triggered, all creatures within 10 feet of the pressure plate must succeed on a DC 12 Dexterity saving throw or take 5d6 bludgeoning damage from the impact of being struck by the dried kernels, which function like shrapnel. The creature takes half as much damage on a successful save. When the husks explode, there is a 50% chance that a monster from **Table 1–3** comes to investigate the commotion within 1d4 rounds of the explosion.

A successful DC 15 Wisdom (Perception) check or Intelligence (Investigation) check locates the pressure plate and the fake husks of maize. A successful DC 15 Dexterity check made with thieves' tools disarms the pressure plate. Each trap incorporates 1d4 + 6 husks into the design. Each husk can be safely removed automatically, though the removal of each individual husk only reduces the bludgeoning damage by 1d3. Obviously deactivating all the husks renders the trap inoperative.

Falling Maize Trap

This devious trap uses a tripwire to cause two wooden poles on opposite walls to fall forward and strike the creature who disturbed the trip wire.

The thin wire is three inches off the ground, and the wooden poles are disguised as maize stalks that are supported by a hinge mechanism that causes each to fall parallel to the tripwire. The trap activates when a creature hits the tripwire. Each wooden pole, which has razor-sharp obsidian shards embedded into its surface, makes a melee attack with a +5 bonus against the creature who triggered the trap or is standing adjacent to the tripwire. Each pole hits the creature closest to it, and the same pole cannot strike more than one creature.

It takes a successful DC 15 Wisdom (Perception) check to spot the tripwire. A successful DC 15 Dexterity check made with thieves' tools severs the tripwire and harmlessly disables the tripwire. A character without thieves' tools can attempt this check with disadvantage using any edged weapon or edged tool. On a failed check, the trap triggers. A character who searches the maize stalks and succeeds on a DC 15 Intelligence (Investigation) check notices the concealed poles and their hinge mechanism, which leads the individual to the tripwire connecting the opposing wooden poles. As an action, a character can tip a pole into the downward position, causing the trap to trigger and strike anyone standing adjacent to the tripwire.

Teleportation Trap

A pressure plate hidden in the ground at the spot marked "T" activates this magical trap. A living creature that steps on the pressure plate and weighs more than 50 pounds triggers the trap.

When a living creature triggers the trap, the target must succeed on a DC 13 Wisdom saving throw or be instantly teleported to a random location 1d6 x 10 feet away from the pressure plate. Because the maize wall is an object, a creature transported into a maize wall appears in an unoccupied space adjacent to the maize wall that is closest to the pressure plate. A spell or other effect that can sense the presence of magic, such as *detect magic*, reveals an aura of conjuration magic around the pressure plate.

A successful DC 15 Wisdom (Perception) check spots the pressure plate, and a successful DC 20 Intelligence (Arcana) check associates the pressure plate with a teleportation device. Wedging a solid object beneath the pressure plate prevents the trap from activating. A successful *dispel magic* (DC 15) cast on the pressure plate destroys the trap.

Area W: Wahuapa

Naturally, a maze created from maize also contains **wahuapas** that blend into the wall and serve as an added line of defense against intruders. These points in the maze designated as "W" are the locations where each of the 4 wahuapas hide within the structure. It takes a successful DC 20 Knowledge (Nature) or Survival check to notice the creature lurking amid the ordinary plants that make up the semi-solid barrier. Because the wahuapas rely upon blindsight, they do not have to actually see the trespasser to detect its presence. When a creature passes within 10 feet of one of these monsters, the maizefolk emerges from the wall and attacks, likely surprising the interloper in the process. The wahuapa fights until destroyed. If a character attempts to communicate with one of these plants, it reacts in the same manner as described in the **Purple Maize** encounter.

Wahuapa   CR 4
XP 1,200
hp 37 (Fields of Blood, "Wahuapa")

Area M1: Ghoulish Delight

These shambling, undead monstrosities congregate in a dead-end in the outermost concentric ring forming the maze. They are the Haunted Maizefield's newest additions, though they frequently enter and exit the structure searching for living prey beyond its boundaries. When the characters come within visual range of their disgusting corner, read or paraphrase the following description:

The filth can be attributed to 6 **ghouls** that inhabit this area of the maze on an apparently temporary basis. The monsters are fairly mobile and move about the complex as well as venturing out of it. Without leadership and direction, the undead horrors mob any creature that wanders into their corner of the maze. They fight without fear, never retreating nor surrendering. If the characters can communicate with the ghouls, they know nothing about the maze's inner workings.

Ghoul (6)   CR 1
XP 400
hp 13 (Pathfinder Roleplaying Game Bestiary, "Ghoul")

Treasure: The ghouls amassed a few baubles among their mounds of refuse, though it takes some digging and a successful DC 10 Perception check to locate a pouch containing 28 cacao beans worth 1 gp each and a *potion of cure light wounds*.

Area M2: Fields of Maize Silk

The vengeful energies of the maizefield summoned these elementals to this forsaken location where they move about the field waiting to slaughter unwanted visitors. The creatures appear to be crafted from the same fibrous plant materials as the wahuapas, which may lead the characters to conclude they share some common ancestry or origin, but the wispy monsters lack the physical substance of the malevolent maizefolk. Despite their seemingly incorporeal nature, they are not skilled at blending into the vegetation or noticing intruders. A character who succeeds on a DC 15 Perception check feels a slight breeze emanating from the nearby gap in the wall. When the characters approach this juncture in the maze, read or paraphrase the following description:

The 5 **bilwises** who inhabit this portion of the maze are remnants from an ancient farmer's long-forgotten grudge. However, they seamlessly blended into the siblings' plans for the site and now reside among their evil brethren. When the monsters notice the characters, they fly forward to attack, moving through the walls to allow some of their ranks to get behind the heroes and flank them. During the first round of combat, each bilwis uses its Whirlwind attack to knock it adversaries off their feet. Until the ability recharges, the elementals slam the characters into submission. If the characters reduce the bilwises' numbers in half, the remaining survivors attempt to flee by flying through the ceiling and into the wilderness outside the maizefield. The monster hides out for several hours before returning to the maizefield to ensure the safety of their accumulated treasures hidden in the surrounding walls. The bilwises' knowledge of the maizefield is limited to the outer concentric rings, though they know a terrible crime took place here and that the resurrected spirits of the children and the man slain here rose from the grave. A character examining the walls from afar must succeed on a DC 20 Perception check to locate their goods. A character who moves through the wall gains a +2 on the preceding check.

Bilwis (5)   CR 1
XP 400
hp 13 (Pathfinder Roleplaying Game Bestiary, "Elemental, Air [Small]")

Treasure: The bilwises keep a *spell of burning hands* and a *cuacalalatli of the beast (eagle)* (see **Appendix C: New Items and Magic**) hidden within the maize.

AREA M3: FUN GUYS

Maize is susceptible to fungi and even the magically manipulated plants that form this enclosure are no exception. If the characters pass through this section of the maze, 8 **phycomids** growing in this section rely upon their tremorsense to detect approaching creatures. Although the fungi initially developed on the plant stalks and leaves, they slowly migrated into the loose soil between the maize walls where they wait for passing prey. When the characters come within visual range of this area, read or paraphrase the following description if a character succeeds on a DC 15 Perception check made to notice the vegetation:

> Tufts of stubby, yellowing grasses protrude from the ground along with tendrils of root material.

If a character takes the time to examine the vegetation and succeeds on a DC 9 Knowledge (Nature) check, that individual determines that the grasses are indeed yellowy strands of fungi. If a creature moves within 10 feet of the phycomids, the monsters uproot themselves from the soil and move forward to attack, lobbing fluid globules at their enemies. The unintelligent phycomids attack until destroyed.

Phycomid (8)   CR 4
XP 1,200
hp 39 (Pathfinder Roleplaying Game Bestiary 2, "Phycomid")

AREA M4: RAGS TO DITCHES

Much like the cacalotls encountered earlier, the inhabitants of this section of the maze appear to be creepy, yet harmless inanimate objects. The creatures have no visual organs, which forces them to rely upon blindsight to detect trespassers approaching their lair. The monsters conceal themselves well among the vegetation in the ceiling above the breach, requiring the heroes to succeed on a DC 25 Perception check to notice them. Unless the characters mention they are looking up at the ceiling, the characters suffer a -2 penalty on the preceding Perception check. When the characters come within visual range of this breach, read or paraphrase the following description:

> A 20-foot-wide gap in the maize walls grants access to adjoining concentric rings.

If a character succeeded on his Perception check, you may add the following detail:

> A sack of linen material shaped into the likeness of a raggedy doll is wedged in place between two adjacent maize stalks in the canopy 13 feet above the ground.

There are 4 **raggedy men** hidden among the vegetation at this critical breach in the maize wall. The devious aberrations attempt to pass themselves off as discarded children's dolls. Indeed, a character who hails from Pilhua notices a striking similarity between the creature and a style of doll popular in the village. However, it is impossible to determine if the creature was once Chipinia's toy that somehow came to life or if the resemblance is a curious coincidence. Regardless, the cunning monsters take advantage of this perception and use their Charm Gaze attack while still affixed to the canopy to charm as many opponents as they can while hurling their Gossamer Strand at characters who resist their charm effect. After spending several rounds attached to a target, the raggedy man severs the tie and drops down from the canopy onto the ground where it resorts to draining its enemy's energy to replenish lost hit points. Despite their cleverness, the monsters are mindless lifeforms that subsist on sapping the vitality of other creatures. The concepts of death, wealth, and motivation do not register with raggedy man's alien mindset. The creatures attack the characters until destroyed.

Raggedy Man (4)   CR 3
XP 800
hp 26 (Fields of Blood, "Raggedy Man")

AREA M5: DROWNING IN SORROW

Under extraordinary circumstances, a child's profound tears of sadness can sometimes spawn unintended consequences. When Conto and Chipinia met their terrifying demise at Mixoch and Temilaz's hands, the tears they shed took on a life of their own as a wicked **tear collector**. The small fiend appears as a humanoid-shaped creature chiseled from rock salt. It dwells at the heart of the maze, likely leading the characters to conclude that it is the cause of the mayhem plaguing the Pilhua. To get inside this section of the maizefield, the heroes must push through the walls or ceiling granting access to the area. When they do so, read or paraphrase the following description:

> A pool of stagnant water sits near the middle of an oval clearing in the maze. Two shrubs with gnarled branches, crimson thorns, and delicate white flowers grow along the pool's edges.

The tear collector loiters near the shallow pool, which is only a few inches deep and contains saline water that feels granular to the touch because of the exceedingly high salt content. The 2 **execrable shrubs** also burrow their roots into the pool's banks even though the plant-like fiends subsist on blood and meat that the tear collector provides it from its available sources. These creatures use their tremorsense ability to detect intruders approaching their secure confines and telepathically communicate the information to the tear collector, who then prepares to blast the trespassers with its acidic tears. The fiendish plants move forward to engage the characters and emit a billowing cloud of smoke that obscures vision. Their tremorsense still allows them to pinpoint the location of opponents in contact with the ground.

Throughout the encounter, the tear collector weeps, sobs, and wails about the injustice committed upon "them" and the "terror of the earth." The fiend further mopes about youth being stolen and the indignity of being shoved into an unmarked grave for no good reason. Despite its excessive lamentation, the monster remains focused on killing the characters and recreating the raw emotions the teenagers experienced during their final moments alive. If the characters converse with the tear collector about the murdered teenagers or any other subject pertaining to the maizefield and its occupants, it blurts out, "fate breathed life into their pathetic spirits and stirred their hatred into palpable anger. Greed sowed these fruits of wrath." The fiend otherwise refuses to respond to questions and provides no further explanation regarding its statement about the perils of avarice. Attempts to coerce it to answer through skill checks automatically fail, though the characters can magically compel it to reply, in which case it reveals Conto and Chipinia's sad story in exacting details as well as their current location within the maze. However, the tear collector has little knowledge of the other creatures inhabiting its lair. The creature's bond to the locale prevents it from fleeing when faced with imminent destruction, a sentiment its newfound shrub companions also share.

Execrable Shrub   CR 1/2
XP 200
hp 5 (Appendix A: New Monsters, "Execrable Shrub")

Tear Collector   CR 5
XP 1,600
hp 39 (Fields of Blood, "Tear Collector")
Treasure: A character notices recently disturbed soil around the pool's edge with a successful DC 15 Perception check. If a creature excavates the area, the individual recovers a wooden box containing *restorative ointment*, a *potion of bull's strength*, a *stone of stunning**, a jar of tlilitl*, and seven garnets worth 100 gp each.

• See **Appendix C: New Items and Magic**

AREA M6: UNREQUITED

One year after their deaths, the teenagers' spirits were reborn as undead monstrosities known as unrequiteds. The youngsters whose blood gave birth to the wahuapas and whose tears conjured the tear collector have no recollection of their former lives. They cannot relay the circumstances of their deaths to the characters and now exist solely to slay every creature that stands in their way. The incorporeal beings appear as wispy, crimson vapors that periodically take the form of an adolescent humanoid. If the characters approach Conto and Chipinia's grave, read or paraphrase the following description:

The siblings' spirits transcended their earthly bodies and transformed into 2 **unrequiteds** that loiter around the grave where Mixoch and Temilaz dumped them more than one year ago alongside Uetzopilli. The incorporeal monsters pass through the maize walls and ceiling without impediment, which allows them to freely move about the area. Although they have no memory of their mortal existence, the undead monsters display some tactical skills. Any creature beholding the ghostly apparitions must first withstand their awful visages, which can stop the most determined adventurers in their tracks. The pair use the maize walls to their advantage, taking withdraw actions to break off combat to reposition themselves in better locations to subject characters to their aura of regret and to physically strike them with their touch. Regardless of the circumstances, they never venture more than 50 feet from their grave and cannot recount any details about their untimely deaths. The siblings can speak, but they limit their conversations to threatening statements and wild boasts.

As previously stated, they remember nothing about their mortal existence and instead focus their malevolent energies on expanding their territory and slaying humanoids. The undead apparitions fight to the end, attacking the heroes mercilessly until they kill their quarry or until the characters end their unnatural existence.

If the characters defeat the ghostly siblings, they are free to explore the grave and retrieve their bodies. Despite being buried for an entire year in a temperate climate with ample moisture, the corpses remain virtually pristine with only mild signs of decomposition. A character who examines the bodies and succeeds on a DC 5 Heal check determines that each sustained puncture wounds to the chest and slashing injuries to the neck. They wear the same clothes they wore on the day they vanished. A successful DC 10 Perception check also locates a broken tecpatl blade and its intact handle. Even casual scrutiny of the weapon reveals that the handle is shaped into the likeness of an ocelot poised to pounce. The weapon belonged to Mixoch, a fact characters can confirm by showing or describing the object to villagers who regularly frequent Pilhua's marketplace.

Despite being incorporeal, the ghostly spirits amassed some items that Uetzopilli's zombie minions hid under the mounds of dirt adjacent to their graves. It is impossible to locate their riches without disturbing the earth and succeeding on a DC 10 Perception check.

Unrequited (2) CR 5
XP 1,600
hp 59 (Marshes of Malice, "Unrequited")

Treasure: Uncovering the loose soil around the grave reveals a golden jaguar statue worth 1,000 gp, a *tangled gourd**, a *rope of climbing*, and *war paint (orange)**.
  • See **Appendix C: New Items and Magic**

Concluding the Adventure

In the aftermath of the unrequiteds' destruction, the maizefield slowly unravels over the next several days as the leaves and stalks forming the roof steadily wane and the walls come undone. The remaining wahuapas go their separate ways to further terrorize Pilhua or other neighboring villages until they are rooted out and vanquished once and for all. If the characters return Conto and Chipinia to the village, Cintecuhtli gives them a proper burial, which gives their grieving family an answer to their long-simmering questions and some measure of closure surrounding their untimely deaths.

If the characters have not already identified Mixoch and Temilaz as the teenagers' killers, the discovery of Mixoch's missing, broken weapon inside the youngsters' grave offers ample proof of at least his guilt. When faced with this evidence, Papalotl has no choice but to dispense the village's brand of frontier justice on the pair or to turn them over to Ixtla's representatives for suitable punishment. The grateful Ciahuatl, if she still lives and if the characters turned her away from evil, profusely thanks the characters for their efforts and dedicates her life to protecting the innocent from harm.

In appreciation for their actions, Pilhua holds a great feast and celebration to honor the heroes who saved their community and unmasked the criminals who perpetrated the horrific crime that set these unfortunately events into motion.

The following new monsters appear in this adventure:

CACALOTL

Cacalotl   CR 3
XP 800
NE Medium construct
Init +2; **Senses** darkvision 60 ft., low-light vision; **Perception** +3

AC 13, touch 12, flat-footed 11 (+2 Dex, +1 natural)
hp 31 (2d10+20)
Fort +0, **Ref** +2, **Will** +1
DR 5/magic; **Immune** construct traits
Weaknesses vulnerability to fire

Speed 30 ft.
Melee 2 claws +3 (1d4 + 1 plus energy drain)
Special Attacks energy drain (1 level, DC 13)
Spell-Like Abilities (CL 2nd; concentration +4)
   1/day—*fear* (DC 15)

Str 12, **Dex** 14, **Con** —, **Int** 8, **Wis** 12, **Cha** 14
Base Atk +2; **CMB** +3; **CMD** 15
Feats Swarm Strike
Skills Stealth +2
SQ freeze

Special Abilities

Freeze (Ex) A cacalotl can hold itself so still it appears to be a doll or scarecrow. A cacalotl that uses freeze can take 20 on its Stealth check to hide in plain sight as a doll or scarecrow.

Swarm Strike +1 to Attacks of Opportunity, +1 for each ally with this feat threatening the target.

EXECRABLE SHRUB

Execrable Shrub   CR 1/2
XP 200
NE Medium plant (evil, extraplanar)
Init +6; **Senses** low-light vision, tremorsense 60 ft.; **Perception** +6

AC 12, touch 12, flat-footed 10 (+2 Dex)
hp 5 (1d8); healed by blood
Fort +2, **Ref** +2, **Will** +2
DR 5/slashing or bludgeoning; **Immune** fire, mind-affecting effects, paralysis, poison, polymorph, sleep, stunning

---

Speed 10 ft., burrow 10 ft.
Melee frond +1 (1d3 + 1 plus 1d6 fire)
Special Attacks heat (1d6 fire)
Spell-Like Abilities (CL 1st; concentration +1)
   Constant—*detect evil*
   1/10 minutes—*obscuring mist*

Str 13, **Dex** 14, **Con** 10, **Int** 3, **Wis** 14, **Cha** 10
Base Atk +0; **CMB** +1; **CMD** 13 (can't be tripped)
Feats Improved Initiative
Skills Acrobatics +2 (-6 to jump), Perception +6
Languages Abyssal, evil telepathy 100 ft.
Special Abilities
Healed by Blood (Su) Whenever a creature dies within 60 feet of the execrable shrub, the shrub regains 5 hp.
Evil Telepathy (100 feet) (Su) Communicate telepathically if the target is evil.

ZOMBIE, GNOLL

Zombie, Gnoll   CR 1
XP 400
NE Medium undead
Init -1; **Senses** darkvision 60 ft.; **Perception** +0

AC 13, touch 9, flat-footed 13 (+2 armor, -1 Dex, +2 natural)
hp 17 (3d8+3)
Fort +1, **Ref** +0, **Will** +3
DR 5/slashing; **Immune** undead traits

Speed 30 ft.
Melee slam +5 (1d6 + 4)

Str 16, **Dex** 8, **Con** —, **Int** —, **Wis** 10, **Cha** 10
Base Atk +2; **CMB** +5; **CMD** 14
Feats Toughness[B]
SQ staggered
Other Gear leather armor

APPENDIX B: NPCs

The following NPCs are found in this adventure:

CINTECUHTLI

Cintecuhtli   CR 4
XP 1,200
Human cleric 5
NG Medium humanoid (human)
Init +1; **Senses** Perception +4

AC 19, touch 11, flat-footed 18 (+6 armor, +1 Dex, +2 shield)
hp 28 (5d8+5)
Fort +6, **Ref** +3, **Will** +9; +2 vs. [electricity] effects or that deal electricity damage

Speed 30 ft. (20 ft. in armor)
Melee tecpatl +2 (1d4 - 1/19-20)
Special Attacks channel positive energy 7/day (DC 14, 3d6)
Domain Spell-Like Abilities (CL 5th; concentration +9)
  7/day—*calming touch* (1d6 + 5), *storm burst* (1d6 + 2 nonlethal)
Cleric Spells Prepared (CL 5th; concentration +9)
  3rd—*call lightning*[D] (DC 17), *prayer, trial of fire and acid* (DC 17)
  2nd—*fog cloud*[D], *resist energy, lesser restoration, sound burst* (DC 16)
  1st—*bless*[D], *enhance water, magic weapon, read weather, shield of faith*
  0 (at will)—*create water, guidance, purify food and drink* (DC 14), *stabilize*
  D Domain spell; **Domains** Community, Weather

Str 8, **Dex** 13, **Con** 12, **Int** 10, **Wis** 18, **Cha** 14
Base Atk +3; **CMB** +2; **CMD** 13
Feats Bless Equipment, Extra Channel, Selective Channeling, Storm-lashed
Skills Acrobatics -2 (-6 to jump), Diplomacy +6, Heal +14 (+15 circumstance to treat wounds or deadly wounds), Knowledge (history) +8, Knowledge (religion) +8, Sense Motive +10, Spellcraft +4
Languages Common
Combat Gear healer's kit; **Other Gear** *+1 olli, +1 light wooden shield*, tecpatl, *cloak of resistance +1*, surgeon's tools

Special Abilities

Bless Equipment Standard Action: Grant single item abilities for 3 rounds.
Calming Touch (1d6 + 5 nonlethal damage, 7/day) (Sp) Heal 1d6 + 5 nonlethal damage and cure conditions by touch.
Storm Burst 1d6 + 2 nonlethal (7/day) (Sp) As a standard action, ranged touch attack deals 1d6 + 2 nonlethal damage to foe in 30 ft. & inflicts a -2 to attack for 1 round.
Storm-Lashed Ignore many of the effects of bad weather.

CIAHUATL

Ciahuatl   CR 4
XP 1,200
Human psychic 5
NE Medium humanoid (human)
Init +1; **Senses** Perception +9

AC 12, touch 12, flat-footed 11 (+1 deflection, +1 Dex)
hp 14 (5d6-4)
Fort +1, **Ref** +3, **Will** +6

Speed 30 ft.
Melee mwk tecpatl +3 (1d4)
Special Attacks painful reminder (1d6, 5/day), phrenic amplifications (mindtouch, overpowering mind), phrenic pool (4 points)
Psychic Spell-Like Abilities (CL 5th; concentration +9)
  1/day—*detect thoughts* (DC 13)
Psychic Spells Known (CL 5th; concentration +9)
  2nd (5/day)—*mind thrust II* (DC 16), *pain strike* (DC 17), *stricken heart*
  1st (7/day)—*cause fear* (DC 16), *ear-piercing scream* (DC 16), *mage armor, persuasive goad* (DC 16), *shield*
  0 (at will)—*dancing lights, detect psychic significance, grave words, open/close* (DC 14), *prestidigitation, telekinetic projectile*
Psychic Discipline Pain

Str 10, **Dex** 13, **Con** 8, **Int** 18, **Wis** 12, **Cha** 14
Base Atk +2; **CMB** +2; **CMD** 14
Feats Empath, Spell Focus (evocation), Spell Focus (necromancy), Subconscious Usurpation
Skills Bluff +10, Diplomacy +10, Intimidate +10, Knowledge (history) +12, Knowledge (local) +12, Knowledge (religion) +12, Perception +9, Sense Motive +9
Languages Common, Draconic, Elven, Gnoll, Sylvan
SQ live on (1d6, 3/day), power from pain (maximum 1)
Other Gear mwk tecpatl, *cloak of resistance +1, ring of protection +1*, 148 gp

Special Abilities

Lay on Hands (1d6 hit points, 3/day) (Su) As a standard action (swift on self), touch channels positive energy and applies mercies.
Mindtouch (Su) 1 pool: detect surface thoughts of spell target (as the 3rd-round effect of detect thoughts).
Overpowering Mind (Ex) 2 pool: increase Will save DC of linked mind-affecting spell by +1.
Painful Reminder 1d6 (5/day) (Su) Swift action: deal nonlethal damage to enemy you damaged with spell on previous or this turn.
Phrenic Pool (4/day) (Su) Pool of points you can use to modify psychic spells as they're cast.
Power From Pain (1/day) (Su) Regain 1 pool when painful reminder does at least 5 damage.
Subconscious Usurpation Will save for mental action while under effect of compulsion, confusion, or possession effect.

JAGUAR WARRIOR

Jaguar Warrior   CR 1
XP 400
Human animal cuauhocelotl (jaguar) fighter 2
LN Medium humanoid (human)
Init +1; **Senses** Perception +0

AC 17, touch 11, flat-footed 16 (+5 armor, +1 Dex, +1 shield)
hp 17 (2d10+6)
Fort +5, **Ref** +1, **Will** +0

Speed 30 ft. (20 ft. in armor)
Melee macuahuitl +5 (1d8 + 3) or
  mwk klar +6 (1d6 + 3)

Str 17, **Dex** 13, **Con** 14, **Int** 8, **Wis** 10, **Cha** 12
Base Atk +2; **CMB** +5; **CMD** 16
Feats Disposable Weapon, Power Attack, Splintering Weapon
Skills Acrobatics +2 (-2 to jump), Climb +4, Craft (weapons) +5, Intimidate +5
Languages Common
Combat Gear *oil of bless weapon, oil of magic weapon, potion of cure light wounds*; **Other Gear** mwk olli, macuahuitl (3), mwk

Animal Cuauhocelotl (Fighter Archetype)

Soldiers who distinguish themselves on the battlefield earn a coveted spot within their homeland's military orders. These martial groups are associated with beasts indigenous to the island. In addition to earning the colorful, distinctive garb affiliated with an order, each of these prestigious organizations offers specialized training to its members that emulate the traits of its beastly namesake. Coyote cuauhocelotls value stealth and resourcefulness. Eagle cuauhocelotls enjoy enhanced perception. Jaguar cuauhocelotls hone their predatory instincts. Serpent cuauhocelotls prize guile and deception. In open battle, each of these orders proudly wears their colorful skins, though coyote cuauhocelotls and serpent cuauhocelotls often hide their allegiance to their order during a clandestine mission.

Bravado. Starting at 2nd level, Tehuatl cuauhocelotls proudly display their courage on the battlefield in an attempt to demoralize their opponents. When you do so, you can use an Attack of Opportunity to lower your guard to an opponent's melee weapon attack against you, granting that opponent a +2 on its attack roll. If the opponent's attack does not reduce you to 0 hit points, impose a condition that prevents you from taking an action, or cause you to become demoralized, the target becomes demoralized. At the end of each of its subsequent turns, the target can make a Will saving throw with a DC of 10 + your Intimidate bonus. On a success, the target is no longer demoralized. If the opponent's initial melee attack missed you, the demoralized foe increases the DC to end the effect to 20 + your Intimidate bonus. You can use this ability a number of times per day equal to an ability score modifier that you use for the Intimidate skill. This replaces Bravery.

Cuauhocelotl Order. At 2nd level, you undergo the rituals and tests required to join an order. Choose one of the following orders:

Coyote: Cleverness and opportunism rank among the coyote cuauhocelotl's prized traits, while discretion may be the better part of valor under less-than-ideal circumstances. Despite the preceding philosophy, abandoning a friend during combat disgraces the order. Spying also comes naturally to the wily coyote. Stealth becomes a class skill for you, and you have a bonus on Stealth checks made while wearing light or no armor equal to half your class level.

Eagle: Keen observation rather than rash reactions win the day. Eagle cuauhocelotls take in their surroundings and then carefully assess every situation. Withdrawal is an acceptable alternative when faced with a superior adversary. An impulsive action that imperils others violates the eagle cuauhocelotl's core values. Eagle cuauhocelotls see what others miss. Perception becomes a class skill for you, and you have a bonus on Perception checks that rely on sight equal to 1/4 your class level.

Jaguar: Preparation is more important than participation. The always calculating jaguar determines when and where to fight. When the time and place are ideal, there can be no surrender nor retreat. With experience, the jaguar cuauhocelotl's predatory senses and agility greatly improve. Acrobatics becomes a class skill for you, and you have a bonus on Acrobatics and Climb checks equal to half your class level.

Serpent. None can defeat you except yourself. Pain offers the path to vanquishing fear. The serpent's scales must be pierced to reveal the cuauhocelotl's true mettle. When the serpent conquers fear, anything becomes possible. Absent the trepidation of failure, trickery and treachery hold the keys to victory. These cuauhocelotls undergo a gruesome scarification ritual that transforms you into a fearless soldier. You regain the Bravery class feature.

Once you select a cuauhocelotl order, you cannot change it. If you commit a transgression that violates the tenets of your order, such as displaying cowardice on the battlefield, you do not gain any additional cuauhocelotl order features until you make amends for your sin by redeeming yourself in battle or through magical redemption such as an *atonement* or similar magic. This replaces your bonus feat at 2nd level.

Improved Cuauhocelotl Order. At 6th level, your cuauhocelotl order bestows the following additional benefits.

Coyote: You learn to attack in the manner of your beastly namesake. You gain 1d6 Sneak Attack damage. This is exactly like the rogue ability of the same name. The extra damage dealt increases by +1d6 every six levels (6th, 12th, and 18th). If a Coyote Cuauhocelotl gets a sneak attack bonus from another source, the bonuses on damage stack.

Eagle: Your visual senses detect the minutest details. You gain the Blind-Fight feat. In addition, you gain Improved Blind-Fight at 12th level and Greater Blind-Fight at 18th level.

Jaguar: You develop the hunting skills of a predatory cat. If you charge at least 20 feet straight toward a creature and then hit it with a melee attack, you may make an additional attack against it with a -5 penalty. At 12th level, you may make a second additional attack with a -10 penalty. At 18th level, you may make a third additional attack at a -15 penalty.

Serpent: You speak with forked tongue and can twist words beyond recognition. Bluff and Disguise becomes class skills for you, and you have a bonus on Bluff and Disguise checks equal to half your class level. Additionally, your Bravery class feature now applies to all Will saving throws.

This replaces your bonus feats at 6th, 12th, and 18th level.

Higher Orders. At 20th level, you become one with your order, reaching the zenith of your orderly powers. Each order gains the following abilities:

Coyote: You can skulk into the background, allowing you to quickly disappear from sight. You gain the rogue talent Hide in Plain Sight for all terrains.

Eagle: Your visual acuity reaches unprecedented heights. You gain constant *see invisibility* as an extraordinary ability.

Jaguar: You master the ability to run down your prey. Your move speed doubles whenever you take the charge or run actions.

Serpent: You master fear and can conquer all. Your Bravery class feature now applies to all attack rolls, ability checks, initiative checks, and saving throws.

This replaces your bonus feat at 20th level.

---

klar, backpack, bedroll, belt pouch, flint and steel, hemp rope (50 ft.), masterwork tool, mess kit, pot, soap, torch (10), trail rations (5), waterskin, 4 gp

Special Abilities

Bravado (1 / day) You can use an Attack of Opportunity to lower your guard to an opponent's melee weapon attack against you, granting that opponent a +2 on its attack roll. If the opponent's attack does not reduce you to 0 hit points, impose a condition that prevents you from taking an action, or cause you to become demoralized, the target becomes demoralized. At the end of each of its subsequent turns, the target can make a Will saving throw with a DC of 10 + your Intimidate bonus. On a success, the target is no longer demoralized. If the opponent's initial melee attack missed you, the demoralized foe increases the DC to end the effect to 20 + your Intimidate bonus.

Mixoch and Temilaz

Mixoch and Temilaz	**CR 3**

XP 800
Human unchained rogue 4
NE Medium humanoid (human)

Init +4; **Senses** Perception +8

AC 16, touch 14, flat-footed 12 (+2 armor, +4 Dex)
hp 22 (4d8+4)
Fort +1, **Ref** +8, **Will** +2
Defensive Abilities danger sense +1, evasion, uncanny dodge

Speed 30 ft.
Melee mwk itztopilli +8 (1d6 + 4)
Special Attacks sneak attack +2d6

Str 8, **Dex** 18, **Con** 10, **Int** 13, **Wis** 12, **Cha** 14
Base Atk +3; **CMB** +2; **CMD** 16
Feats Combat Expertise, Feint Partner, Improved Feint, Twinned Feint, Weapon Finesse
Skills Acrobatics +11, Bluff +9, Diplomacy +6, Disable Device +15, Disguise +6, Escape Artist +11, Intimidate +6, Knowledge (dungeoneering) +5, Knowledge (local) +8, Perception +8, Sense Motive +8, Sleight of Hand +11, Stealth +11
Languages Common, Gnoll
SQ debilitating injury: bewildered, debilitating injury: disoriented, debilitating injury: hampered, rogue talents (combat trick, mien of despair), trapfinding +2

Combat Gear *elixir of hiding, potion of invisibility*; **Other Gear**
+1 ichcahuipilli, mwk itztopilli, *sleeves of many garments*,
concealable thieves' tools

Special Abilities

Debilitating Injury: Bewildered -2/-4 (Ex) Foe who takes sneak
  attack damage takes AC penalty (more vs. striker) for 1 round.
Debilitating Injury: Disoriented -2/-4 (Ex) Foe who takes sneak
  attack damage takes attack penalty (more vs. striker) for 1
  round.
Debilitating Injury: Hampered (Ex) Foe who takes sneak attack
  damage has speed halved (and can't 5 ft step) for 1 round.
Feint Partner When ally successfully feints, opponent loses Dex
  bonus against your next attack
Improved Feint You can make a Bluff check to feint in combat as a
  move action.
Mien of Despair (Su) When demoralize or feint foe, can't benefit
  from morale bonuses for 1d4 + 1 rounds.
Twinned Feint As a move action, attempt feint vs. a foe in reach,
  if successful make an add feint vs. adjacent foe, -2 AC until next
  of turn.

PAPALOTL

Papalotl   CR 4
XP 1,200
Middle-aged human fighter (tribal fighter) 5
N Medium humanoid (human)
Init +2; **Senses** Perception +0

AC 21, touch 11, flat-footed 20 (+8 armor, +1 Dex, +2 shield)
hp 38 (5d10+10)
Fort +6, **Ref** +4, **Will** +2 (+1 vs. fear)

Speed 30 ft. (20 ft. in armor)
Melee mwk itztopilli +9 (1d6 + 6), mwk klar +7 (1d6 + 1)
Special Attacks weapon training (tribal +1)

Str 16, **Dex** 14, **Con** 12, **Int** 13, **Wis** 11, **Cha** 9
Base Atk +5; **CMB** +8; **CMD** 20
Feats Improved Shield Bash, Improved Unarmed Strike, Power
  Attack, Shield Focus, Two-weapon Fighting, Weapon Focus
  (itztopilli), Weapon Specialization (itztopilli)
Skills Acrobatics -4 (-8 to jump), Craft (carpentry) +12, Craft
  (weapons) +11, Profession (soldier) +10, Survival +8
Languages Common, Elven
SQ armor training 1, battle focus, forbidden armor
Combat Gear *potion of cure moderate wounds, potion of enlarge
  person, potion of shield of faith*; **Other Gear** mwk ollixalli, mwk
  itztopilli, mwk klar, *cloak of resistance +1, traveler's any-tool*, 34 gp

Special Abilities

Tribal Weapon Training (Ex) Feats that affect a specific weapon in
  tribal weapon group, affect them all.
Weapon Training (Tribal) +1 (Ex) +1 Attack, Damage, CMB, CMD
  with Tribal weapons

TRIBAL WARRIOR

Tribal Warrior   CR 1/2
XP 200
Human fighter (tribal fighter) 1
LN Medium humanoid (human)
Init +2; **Senses** Perception +1

AC 17, touch 12, flat-footed 15 (+4 armor, +2 Dex, +1 shield)
hp 9 (1d10+3)
Fort +4, **Ref** +2, **Will** +1

Speed 30 ft. (20 ft. in armor)

Melee klar +3 (1d6 + 2) or shortspear +4 (1d6 + 2) or
  unarmed strike +3 (1d3 + 2)

Str 15, **Dex** 15, **Con** 14, **Int** 10, **Wis** 12, **Cha** 8
Base Atk +1; **CMB** +3; **CMD** 15
Feats Improved Unarmed Strike, Power Attack, Weapon Focus
  (shortspear)
Skills Acrobatics -1 (-5 to jump), Climb +3, Survival +5, Swim +3
Languages Common
SQ battle focus, forbidden armor
Combat Gear *potion of cure light wounds* (4); **Other Gear** mwk
  hide armor, klar, shortspear (5), backpack, bandolier, bedroll, belt
  pouch, flint and steel, torch (10), trail rations (4), waterskin, 3 sp

VENLO INNOVA

Venlo Innova   CR 1
XP 400
Gnome alchemist (mindchemist) 2
CG Small humanoid (gnome)
Init +2; **Senses** low-light vision; Perception +8

AC 16, touch 13, flat-footed 14 (+3 armor, +2 Dex, +1 size)
hp 13 (2d8+4)
Fort +5, **Ref** +5, **Will** +1; +2 vs. illusions and poison
Defensive Abilities defensive training

Speed 20 ft.
Melee mwk gnome pincher +1 (1d4 - 2)
Ranged bomb +5 (1d6 + 2 fire)
Special Attacks bomb 4/day (1d6 + 2 fire, DC 13), hatred
Spell-Like Abilities (CL 2nd; concentration +3)
  1/day—*dancing lights, ghost sound* (DC 12), *prestidigitation,
  speak with animals*
Alchemist (Mindchemist) Extracts Prepared (CL 2nd;
  concentration +4)
  1st—*crafter's fortune* (DC 13), *identify, tears to wine* (DC 13)

Str 6, **Dex** 14, **Con** 15, **Int** 15, **Wis** 12, **Cha** 12
Base Atk +1; **CMB** -2; **CMD** 10
Feats Amateur Investigator, Brew Potion, Throw Anything
Skills Acrobatics +2 (-2 to jump), Craft (alchemy) +11 (+13 to
  create alchemical items), Heal +6, Knowledge (arcana) +9,
  Knowledge (nature) +9, Perception +8, Spellcraft +7, Use Magic
  Device +6; **Racial Modifiers** +2 Craft (alchemy), +2 Perception
Languages Common, Dwarven, Elven, Gnome, Sylvan
SQ alchemy (alchemy crafting +2), cognatogen (+4/-2, +2 natural
  armor, 20 minutes), discovery (glitterbomb), gnome magic,
  perfect recall
Other Gear mwk hide shirt, mwk gnome pincher, *traveler's any-
  tool*, alchemist starting formula book, masterwork backpack

Special Abilities

Amateur Investigator (2/day) You gain a pool of inspiration equal to
  your Intelligence modifier. You can expend one use of inspiration
  as a free action to add 1d6 to the result of a Knowledge,
  Linguistics, or Spellcraft check, as long as you are trained in that
  skill (even if you take 10 or 20 on that check). You make this
  choice after the check is rolled and before the results of the roll
  are revealed. You can use inspiration only once per skill check.
Cognatogen (DC 13) (Su) Mutagen adds +4 to a mental & -2 to a
  physical attribute, and +2 nat. armor for 20 minutes.
Glitterbomb (DC 13) The bomb covers all creatures within its
  area (including targets of splash damage) in a cloud of golden
  particles, visibly outlining invisible things for 1 round / level.
  Creatures in the area may make Reflex saves to reduce the
  duration of the glittering effect to 1 round. Any creatures
  covered by the dust take a -40 on Stealth checks.
Perfect Recall At 2nd level, a mindchemist has honed his memory.
  When making a Knowledge check, he may add his Intelligence
  bonus on the check a second time.

Appendix C: New Items and Magic

The following weapons, armor, and magic items are found in this adventure:

New Armor

Nonetheless, the bulk of the new armor and shields presented below adheres to the principles of providing lightweight defensive options without compromising stealth and mobility.

Light Armor

This defensive equipment typically consists of thin, flexible material stitched together in layers to provide stopping power against projectiles and sharp implements as well as deadening the impact of bludgeoning weapons that strike the armor.

Ichcahuipilli. This two-inch-thick light armor resembles a vest designed to protect the wearer's torso from the neck to the hips against arrows and sharp blades. It consists of layers of cotton and vegetable fiber stitched together in a network of interconnected diamond-shaped patterns and then soaked in brine or another saline solution to harden the materials.

Medium Armor

Protective gear falling into this category provides added defense at the expense of mobility. Supple materials are generally combined with more rigid, durable components to allow the wearer to better fend off attacks while not bogging him down with overly heavy gear.

Olli. Armor smiths combine latex and the juice from a morning glory vine to create a flexible and resilient material resembling modern rubber. Although typically used to create the tlatchli, clever innovators use the durable substance to protect warriors from injury. The lightweight suit includes a jacket and leggings. An inner and outer lining of breathable linen provides added comfort. While wearing this armor, you reduce any falling damage you take by 5 points, though you cannot reduce the falling damage below 0. Because it is made from plant-based products, druids are permitted to wear olli, and it is immune to rust. Furthermore, you are not considered to be wearing medium armor against the effects the extreme heat.

Heavy Armor

Those willing to sacrifice mobility and comfort for added protection ultimately turn to heavy armor. This category of defensive equipment covers the entire body with hard, sturdy materials with the strength to deflect projectiles and even powerful blows from a melee weapon.

Ollixalli. One day, Atoyapaca, an innovative botanist and renowned jeweler heated olli and combined it with ground quartz to enhance its strength. His bold experiment exceeded his wildest expectations, leading others to follow in its footsteps by adding other silica-based and sulfurous components to the liquified olli mixture. The delicate and laborious process of creating ollixalli is a tightly guarded secret confined to those who have the technical expertise and specialized equipment required to set the ollixalli mold. Unlike conventional heavy armor, a suit of ollixalli consists of a lightweight jacket and pants that protect the torso and limbs. Ollixalli has no metal components, making it suitable for druids and immune to rust. While wearing ollixalli armor, you are not considered to be wearing heavy armor against the effects of extreme heat. Because of the specialized training and equipment needed to create ollixalli, the armor remains extremely expensive and rare.

> ### Keep it Simple or Realistic?
>
> The following sections present new armor and weapons that share many similarities yet have some noteworthy differences from commonly found armor and weapons. You have two options when dealing with the new armor and weapons presented here. You can choose to keep this section simple by retaining the descriptive entries for the armor and weapons while assigning them the same game statistics and costs as existing armor. Alternatively, you can use the costs, game statistics, and special abilities presented below in their entirety. It is recommended that you adopt a consistent approach to handling the armor and weapons rather than treating some items as currently existing armor and weapon types while incorporating the special rules for other items. If you opt for the simple choice, the equivalent existing item appears as the last entry in **Tables C–1** and **C–2**.

New Weapons

Itztopilli. This axe has a wooden haft with a bronze head fitted into a groove built into the haft. The head is long and narrow, and its cutting surface is only slightly wider than the axe's flat back. The itztopilli's versatile design allows you to hack into flesh as well as chop wood with remarkable accuracy and comparable ease. Indeed, most woodworkers incorporate the weapon into a standard set of carpenter's tools. If you are proficient with the itztopilli, and you made an attack roll with the weapon within the last 24 hours, you also gain a +1 circumstance bonus to Craft (carpentry).

Macuahuitl. Made from hardwood such as oak, this weapon resembles a long, flat paddle with obsidian or flint chips embedded into the weapon's edges. The insertion of these incredibly sharp stones gives the weapon unmatched cutting power at the cost of increased fragility. When you attack a creature with this weapon and roll a 20 on the attack roll, you score a critical hit as normal and deal an extra effect if the attack roll confirms against the target by 10 or more. The

Table C–1: Tehuatl Armor

Armor	Cost	Armor Bonus	Max Dexterity Bonus	Armor Check Penalty	Arcane Spell Failure Chance	Speed (30 ft. base)	Weight	Equivalent
Light Armor								
Ichcahuipilli	15 gp	+1	+8	0	5%	30 ft.	4 lbs.	padded
Medium Armor								
Olli	75 gp	+5	+3	-4	25%	20 ft.	12 lbs.	scale mail
Heavy Armor								
Ollixalli	1,000 gp	+8	+0	-7	40%	20 ft.	25 lbs.	half plate

Weapon	Cost	Damage (Medium)	Critical	Range	Weight	Type	Special	Equivalent
Simple Light Melee Weapons								
Itztopilli	4 gp	1d6	x2	—	2 lbs.	S	see text	Handaxe
Tecpatl	2 gp	1d4	x2	—	1 lb.	P or S	fragile, see text	Dagger
Martial One-Handed Melee Weapons								
Macuahuitl	10 gp	1d8	x2	—	2 lbs.	S	fragile, see text	Longsword

creature struck takes 1d8 bleed damage at the start of each of its turns due to the blade gouging a deep laceration through the creature's flesh. The bleed damage increases by 1d8 if you inflict another deep laceration during a subsequent attack.

Tecpatl. Carved from flint or obsidian, this double-edged knife has a pointed tip and a decorative wooden, stone, or mosaic handle. Although an effective, close-quarters combat weapon, the tecpatl is predominately used in religious rites and revered for its multitude of symbolic roles. When used in battle, it may open a deep laceration in the same manner as described under the **macuahuitl** entry (see above).

EQUIPMENT

Copal Glue **(100 gp; 1lb.)** When mixed, this amalgamation of cooked resin from copal and pine trees creates a strong and durable adhesive. When found, a container of this glue contains 1d6 + 1 ounces of the substance. One ounce of the glue can cover a 1-foot-square surface. It takes 1d4 + 1 rounds to set. You can use the glue to help repair a damaged or broken item. When you use the glue in this manner, you gain a +2 alchemical bonus on the check to repair the object. When applied to a surface that can be opened, such as a door, lid, or gate, the object is more difficult to force open; the DC to pry the object open increases by 1d4 + 1. The bond lasts indefinitely, though once a bonded surface is forced open, or a paired object becomes broken again, the glue is destroyed.

Iyollo **(75 gp)** A creature that drinks this delicious, chocolate-flavored drink experiences exhilaration and euphoria for one hour. Whenever you fail a Will saving throw, you do not suffer the effects from the failed saving throw until the end of your next turn. Until then, you are aware of the failed saving throw's potential consequences and may take actions to counteract its effects. In addition, you have a +2 alchemical bonus on Will saving throws made to end an ongoing spell or effect, when applicable.

Tlilitl **(25 gp)** A creature that drinks this vial of vanilla-flavored liquid with hints of chocolate gains a +2 alchemical bonus on saving throws against being put to sleep by magic for one hour.

MAGIC ITEMS

BALCHÉ

Aura faint divination; **CL** 3rd; **Slot** —; **Price** 1,000 gp; **Weight** —
This mildly intoxicating concoction is a mixture of tree bark soaked in honey and water. When found, a vial contains 1d4 + 1 one-ounce doses of the fermented liquid. You can use a standard action to drink a dose. The effects last for 10 minutes. When you do so, you gain a greater understanding of nature. You have a +2 alchemical bonus on Knowledge (nature) checks and Charisma checks made when interacting with creatures with the Fey type. While in the outdoors where nature has not been replaced by construction, such as a town or the interior of a building, you ignore difficult terrain and cannot be surprised. When crafted, the vial contains all 5 doses.

Feats Craft Wondrous Item; **Spells** *enhanced diplomacy*; **Price** 500 gp

CUACALALATLI OF THE BEAST

Aura faint transmutation; **CL** 7th; **Slot** head; **Price** 16,000 gp; **Weight** 2 lbs.
These wooden helmets are shaped into the likenesses of various beast heads. The protective device fits over your head and covers the top and back of your skull as well as your jawline. While wearing this helmet, you gain its abilities. The type of beast associated with the helmet determines its specific properties.

Eagle: You are constantly aware of your surroundings, even in the thick of combat. You cannot be surprised. When you are hit by an attack that deals extra damage, you can use your immediate action to reduce the attack's extra damage by 1d10 + your Dexterity modifier (minimum of 0). If you reduce the extra damage to 0, you ignore any other effect that the extra damage normally causes.

Feats Craft Wondrous Item;

Spells *beast shape II*;

Price 8,000 gp STONE OF STUNNING

Aura strong enchantment; **CL** 15th; **Slot** —; **Price** 5,000 gp; **Weight** —
Made from hard rubber, these spherical sling stones are designed to debilitate rather than kill an enemy. When you hit a creature with the stone, the stone deals 1 bludgeoning damage instead of normal damage. The target must succeed on a DC 22 Fortitude saving throw or be stunned. At the end of each of its turns, a creature stunned by the stone may make another Fortitude saving throw. On a success, the creature is no longer stunned.

Once a stone deals damage to a creature, it becomes a nonmagical stone. Other types of magic ammunition of this kind exist, such as rubber-tipped *arrows of stunning* or *bolts of stunning*, though stones are the most common variety.

Feats Craft Magical Arms and Armor; **Spells** *power word stun*; **Price** 2,500 gp

TANGLED GOURD

Aura faint transmutation; **CL** 1st; **Slot** —; **Price** 150 gp; **Weight** 1 lb.
This roughly spherical green, orange, or bright yellow gourd is three inches in diameter and weighs one pound. You can use a standard action to throw the gourd up to 40 feet. The gourd rips apart on impact and fills the area with fibrous vines for one minute. Each creature within a 10-foot radius of where the gourd lands must succeed on a DC 12 Reflex saving throw or be entangled by the vines. The affected area becomes difficult terrain. A creature that enters the affected area for the first time or an unentangled creature that starts its turn in the affected area must succeed on a DC 12 Reflex saving throw to avoid being entangled. A creature already entangled by the vines at the start of its turn takes 2d6 bludgeoning damage. A creature restrained by the vines can use a standard action to free itself. To do so, it must succeed on a DC 12 Strength or Escape Artist check. When the vines disappear after one minute, all entangled creatures are freed, and the affected area reverts to whatever terrain it was before the vines appeared.

Feats Craft Wondrous Item; **Spells** *entangle*; **Price** 75 gp

WAR PAINT

Aura moderate varies; **CL** 9th; **Slot** —; **Price** 9,000 gp; **Weight** —
Typically stored in clay jars two inches in diameter, each container holds 1d3 applications of viscous pigments made from dyes and other colorful components. Each jar contains one color of paint, and its contents weigh half a pound. As a standard action, one dose of war paint can be rubbed onto the skin. The pigment covers roughly six square inches of skin. A creature can wear no more than three different colors of paint at a time, and you cannot simultaneously apply the effects of more than one color of *war paint* to the same weapon. Any attempt to apply more than three colors of war paint fails. Each application of paint lasts for 10 minutes regardless of color. The *war paint*'s color determines its effects. When crafted each container contains 3 applications of the same color.

Orange: You never back down and thrive when the odds are stacked against you. You are immune to fear. If two or more hostile creature are within five feet of you at the start of your turn, you may use your swift action to make a melee attack against one of the hostile creatures if it is within reach.

Feats Craft Wondrous Item; **Spells** *heroism* (orange); **Price** 4,500 gp